3 - 11 - 19

The Last Enchantment

Dear Jessica,

Happy Reading

I hope you enjoy the book.

Raju

The sword and shield of light with the magic potion pot

Vt vas gladius veneno magicis lux

ISBN: 1500708291

ISBN: 9781500708290

Library of Congress Control Number: 2015901166

CreateSpace Independent Publishing Platform

North Charleston, South Carolina

The Adventures of Tom McGuire

The Last Enchantment

Volume 4

RAYNER TAPIA

Acknowledgments

Literary Laureates

"In all adversity, ride the tide and let
the creativity flow"
Rayner Tapia

"Logic will get you from A to B.
Imagination will get you everywhere."
Albert Einstein

"The difficulty of literature is not to write,
but to write what you mean."
Robert Louis Stevenson

"All the best stories in the world are but one
story in reality—the story of escape.
It is the only thing which interests us all
and at all times, how to escape."
Arthur Christopher Benson

"We read to know we are not alone."
C.S. Lewis

"Believe you can and you're halfway there."
Theodore Roosevelt

In Loving Memory of My Dad

Thank you to my wonderful family.
And to my brilliant sisters. Thank you.

Thank you, Mr. George Ruddock,
for your ineffable support.

Thank you Carole Marblestein (my president-ness)
for your ongoing support.

Thank you Cllr. James Bond for being
my publicity extraordinaire.

Shukri, who is my shadow, my friend from the core,
who gave me the confidence and encouragement
to write even more.

To the many friends and people I have met on this journey.
Thank you.

To my Mum, for everything you do

OBLIVIONARA

OLD
OAK TREE

RIPPLE M.

ORACLE

PALA
OF GREA

MOUNTAINS OF
THE MOON

H.

WISHING
WELL

GRIMMS
MARSH

BOILER
ROOM

SS

DEMON C

MARSHES

TOWER OF
BELLE Á NOIR

MORIADIYA

CLE

CLOMP OF
TUMBLEWOOD

COURT OF
PRYTONEUM

Contents

Chapter I
A Misconception

Everything seemed to display a sense of normality, but for Tom and James, it was anything but normal. Their lives had already changed since the discovery of the dominion worlds.

Thus for each day, each month, and each year that would pass, their deep guarded secret became enshrined in their very existence. They grew older, wiser, knowing that they would always be pursued by the demon princess Morkann. She was driven by a deep dislike of anything that did not comply with her world, consumed with such hatred it was disturbing. Her wild emotion and the strength of her indignation did not falter. It was their quest to stay alive whilst protecting their Mother, the secret, they held undiscovered.

During the first few years since their last visit to the extra-terrestrial world, life had become an adventure. They knew their lives would never return to simply existing. James and Tom had now grown to become young athletic men, adolescents, strong and handsome, and perhaps even proud they were the sons of an extra-terrestrial Mother.

It seemed they were destined to a life in which every path, every wilderness, and every mountain they climbed would lead them to Morkann's wrath. Their childhood had past, and with the revelation that their own Mother belonged to a planet, which they had discovered, a new chapter begun.

They were from the McGuire household, unknown young princes from a Mother who was from an outer galactic planet, and although their daily routines were sometimes obscure and mundane most of the time they carried out the habitual things that anyone else would do.

However, in all this normality, the two brothers were different, not in appearance but how they would conduct themselves in everyday situations. They were hard working – yes, but they were secretive. The secret they held could not be shared; neither would they ever want to disclose it. If they did they would risk being ridiculed by their peers and more importantly being harassed by the police force or MI5 or perhaps even the FBI for withholding secretive information. It was a time when humans sought life outside planet Earth and their quest for life or any life forms in the galactic airspace. Scientists from all over the world were insisting there was terrestrial life to be found, even though no life had been discovered.

The secret was their Mother, Lindiarna. Their secret, once exposed would unleash a complete world-wide frenzy of interest toward their Mother. Lindiarna who was from the outer space planet, Oblivionarna sought refuge on planet Earth and had done so for a very long time. Human scientists from all over planet Earth had sought to discover any life outside their dominion. They were desperate to outwit anyone who could ascertain a new planet containing a life source; little did they know that here on Earth itself resided an extra-terrestrial, who took the appearance of a woman, Mother of two adolescents going to college! Her life had been transformed into a 'very human' way of existence ever since she had adopted life on Earth as her own, but the extra-terrestrial demon Morkann still waited for the demise of Lindiarna in order for her to take full control of the planet Oblivionarna, which she had left behind. This was the planet, which James and Tom had discovered from their previous visits. The characters they had met advised them of their perils; and quest of their awaiting roles as future princes. However, it was known should Lindiarna return she was to be crowned queen, the true queen from another world — a parallel world — an Andromeda galaxy.

This was the planet both young men had visited and now it was time to revisit the planet once more as they were older and were aware of the dangers.

The two young men were to return to the planet to finally reclaim their throne away from the evil clutches of Morkann – better known as 'Temperatia', the demon princess.

It had been a few years since the boys had visited the planets in the dark outer galactic airspace making new discoveries. They were each time, mesmerized by the constellation of stars and the enchanting beings that they would meet.

Lindiarna was destined to be the Queen of Oblivionarna and all the dominion lands, but not without peril; she slowly realised if she was to revisit the land and claim her throne she would have no choice but to forfeit her life. Her thoughts darted around her mind while her turmoil and anguish consumed her. Her face etched the creases of an old oil painting.

The Andromeda galaxies were the planets beyond the darkness of space and time, where it would lose its continuity. The Earth's human scientists could never fathom that these planets, if discovered would have life in the form of Kings and Queens together with many other creatures, let alone an alien Queen walking on planet Earth. The questions the boys would ask frequently about the planets and their involvement befuddled their already daunted minds, but James was trying to make sense of this inscrutable mystery as to why their Mother did not wish to return to her land of birth and why was Morkann their enemy, filled with so much anger and rage? Her world was dark and treacherous. It was known in the dominion lands that Morkann was their enemy, and she would never let Lindiarna and her offspring take the throne to the planet of Oblivionarna.

These two planets, Oblivionarna and Moradiya were from outer galactic space and beyond, the world that humans wanted to discover – but never could. Although, the human race tried to discover these planets within the Milky-Way, they only seemed to get as far as the Red planet and did not see the Rainbow Nebulas of life. They were a kaleidoscope of lands, undiscovered, which James and Tom had stumbled upon through hidden passages and links, locating various routes that eventually would lead them to find their Mother's true identity. This was Lindiarna's bequest and their orgin was indeed their very own destiny.

The time was right; both young men were eligible princes now, and Morkann was in a precarious predicament. She could not lose this battle if she was to retain the stolen throne. It was imperative that James should visit the strange lands once more and not Tom, as he was the oldest of two young men and he had secured a deep friendship with the Unicorns and Princess Anna-Lisa who could lead him through the harsh terrain. Indeed, his visit to the lands was vital to return to the galaxies to eventually reclaim their throne finally away from the pernicious clutches of Morkann who was still under the illusion that she had taken the throne since the death of kind King Cepheus, Lindiarna's father. He had tried in all his capacity to protect the young princess Lindiarna hence he banished her to planet Earth for her wellbeing.

James felt a sudden pain grip his rib cage, he lunged forward grabbing his stomach in agony, "argh, what is happening?" He moaned trying desperately and discreetly to suppress his pain. The enemy was near and had returned. James knew it would not be long before he would have to leave for the planets.

The pain intensified and stopped him, in his tracks as if he was thrown off a horse. He now had to get back home and quickly. Morkann had returned to stop them leaving for the planets. She was always one step ahead. Feeling the sharp pain intensify in his stomach he comprehended it was Morkann. She was known for her malevolent energy and malicious spells, causing him to fall weak. Morkann comprehended that James was the first heir after Lindiarna, so she would do anything to rid the planets of him. "Hush!" said James, "she is here somewhere near...I can feel it." He said to Tom looking at his immediate surroundings anxiously.

"Come on, we can't say here" pleaded James.

Although James was in pain one hand was still holding his stomach and the other had his bag, which was slumped over his shoulder. He called out to his brother, "Tom, I think we are going to have to leave to visit those lands", James suggested reluctantly.

"Ok", Tom nodded. "Are you ok? What's happened to you? And "Why are you holding your stomach?" Tom asked.

"I'll explain later come on, the quicker we get out of here the sooner we can get home. You know we are going to have to take Mom with us this time and get to those lands". James Suggested as he held his stomach.

"Yes, I know! Are you alright?" asked Tom again.

"Yes I am!" replied James

"Well, you don't look it," Tom said agitated. Tom gave James a deep stare fumed with frustration.

"What is it? Why're you looking at me like that?" said James.

"I know you're going back to find her and I know you liked her."

"Who are you talking about?"

"But you wouldn't do anything stupid, would you?"

"What do you mean?"

"Well, that princess! The one you were goo-eyed about for ages!"

"Oh that one... yes...look, she was important, but I don't know where she is and I don't know where the Unicorn is either." protested James.

"Ok, you just seemed inseparable." Tom moaned.

"What's your point? I left her with the Unicorn and the others. I just hope they survived," snapped James.

Tom sighed, looking defeated.

They looked at each other. His own brother would not divulge anything about the princess he had met. Yet, Tom felt he had no idea what he would do next.

"Drop it Tom, I've got a feeling something is about to happen!"

"I know Morkann's back!" James blurted.

"How do you know?" queried Tom.

"I just do! Now come on," James replied frustrated.

Both brothers were finishing for the day from their lessons at Green College.

As they both began to quicken their pace and walk out of the college, James tried to recall Jambalee's words of strength. Jambalee was an extra-terrestrial being, who he had met when he had visited the land. He was a Lupan leader of a formidable character with a strange appearance. He always wore a tall triangular green wizard's hat, which resembled a cucumber, but it was bent containing several creases until it reached the tip, where it pointed so fine that it almost disappeared. His trousers were green and ill-fitting accompanying a purple tail coat, which looked as if it was too long and tight it was all held together with a single brown wooden button. He was a loyal servant to Lindiarna and King Cepheus. James first met him when he found the planets and he helped him rescue Princess Anna-Lisa imprisoned in Morkann's tower of death, '*Belle á Noir*.' It was here he would guide James out of the pit of hell where the Unicorns perished to their demise.

He was always there to provide guidance and assistance in the weird worlds the brothers had exposed. James quickly turned to Tom,

"Tom have you still got the shield of life', potion pot and the encrusted sword Jambalee gave you?

"Well yes . . . I think so. It's it my wardrobe, somewhere — why? James you're still in pain?" Tom asked with an incredulous look about him.

"No, I am fine, I'll be okay, come on" James said releasing his hand over his torso for a second, trying to convince his brother he was well. He scrunched up his eyes and gazed at his brother.

"Tom I need you to bring all of those items, especially that potion pot. We are going to need them, I am sure." James said.

Tom looked befuddled. "James, have you got a plan?"

"Yes, but don't worry. . . come on, don't worry, just watch. I know SHE is back! The quicker we get to Mom the better".

"Did you see her? And I know you are in pain!" Tom was persistent but James still did not answer.

He looked at his brother who subserviently followed him, listening to every word.

"Look at me Tom!" said James.

Tom looked straight into his eyes. James held his gaze for a moment in silence.

Then his face become softer and the pain had subsequently disappeared. He felt he was able to release his hand from his stomach, and the shadow of a suppressed smile slowly appeared.

"Tom you know, I don't need to see that THING in order for me to know she is here" snapped James furiously referring to Morkann.

James would often frequently remember the characters he had met on his visit to the planets. The creatures he recalled were close to him when he met them on the flamboyant planets. But the image of Morkann was too prominent; he regularly recalled her devilish hair, dagger nails and her wide eyes cold as stone.

The dark wrath of Morkann continues, as her malovent evil falls to shroud the Earth moon.

Tenebris ira Morkann pergit, ut ad eam malovent malum incidit operiam terram luna

The hair on his neck shot up like spikes on a porcupine's back as if it were to commence for battle.

"Come on, Tom; hurry up. Let's get out of here. I have a feeling that something is about to happen!" barked James.

Tom stood still, bewildered in the corridor, with his blue eyes wide open and alert. He hurriedly gathered pace toward the two front exit doors.

Who knew that after all this time Morkann, the demon princess, would resurface, with no warning? James's intuition had become stronger; he could now feel that something was clearly not right and something quite ambiguous was about to happen. James rushed through the corridor with Tom scurrying behind him like a lost mouse in panic.

"Wait up… James, Tell me what's wrong. What's happened? What did you see?"

Tom questioned eagerly. He was worried, he frowned, dipping his brow still darting along with James toward the exit doors.

"Ok, if you really have to know, she is here? We are going to have to get home and quick to check if Mom is okay? You will have to find the sword and shield!" James said, hurrying in pursuit of the exit doors.

As they hurried into the crowd of students all leaving the building at the same time, a bottleneck formed near the exit. The boys knew they were close. They seemed to pass all of their friends hoping they would not be stopped. However, Tom was halted by one of his classmates. His friend, Adam Holmes pushed out his hand, grabbing Tom's forearm as he tried to rush past.

"Hey, Tom, will you be out tonight? Where are you going, in such a rush? "

Adam was lucky he had managed to get a hold of Tom. He was now walking alongside an anxious Tom toward the front doors. He was one of Tom's close friends, as well as being the top student in physics; everyone wanted to be his friend. He was athletic, tall, and strong, with a charismatic face. He had short brown wavy hair, which was almost curly. His face was overpowered with huge, ocean-blue eyes and long, thick black eyelashes. He was a school heart throb. Although Tom never told him about his adventures or the discoveries of the planets he had visited, Adam had a deep suspicion of Tom and his brother.

None of the other students in the college had any idea about Tom or James, but it was a known fact that something was strange about the two brothers, and they did hold something back from everyone. It was their secret – and no one knew.

Adam wanted to befriend Tom, who was, in his mind, an intelligent companion. Adam also found him to be an interesting young character with lots to tell, but only to his friends—Adam thought he might become one of the brother's closest friends.

"No, I don't think I will tonight, Adam, but I'll see you around—yes," Tom said, biting the corner of his mouth as he turned away.

James gritting his teeth stared at the path out of the college. He yelled again through the corridor, his voice reverberating from one end to the other of the long passageway, bouncing off the walls to encourage Tom to speed up.

"Come on, Tom!" yelled James.

In his frustration to leave the college, James rubbed his forehead, anxiously and began to feel apprehensive of the imminent encounter with Morkann.

"I am coming—goodness!"

Tom rolled his eyes, stomping his feet as he hurriedly galloped toward James. He was now trying to ignore his friends, who were all trying to get a hold of him as he rushed past.

Once the two boys were together, they quickened their pace to exit the college. They were running past everyone, scurrying out like mice being chased by a hungry cat from the college at great speed.

"What's happened?" questioned Tom, irritated, trying to fathom out exactly what had happened.

"I'll tell you later. I just need to confirm it first. Come on; let's just get out of here quickly. I think the time has come Tom!"

James, aghast and unsettled, continued to run towards the oversized exit doors. But his mind was frantically darting from one thought to another, and for some reason the exit doors seemed farther away and still at some distance. They continued to run through the clinical, sterile corridors packed with students. Then they could see their path become clear, until they could see the great wide oak doors suddenly zoom up in front of them.

This was it; they were almost at the exit.

Both young men were now practically out of the college, and James was losing his breath, he stopped for a moment, thinking about the enormity of the task ahead. He looked up, squeezing his eyes in anticipation, staring all around him. There he could see the sinister, stormy clouds appear through the large Velux roof windows, looming overhead like a thick blanket, blocking out what little illumination the day moon had provided. He heard a wild raven caw in the distance, almost as if its piercing wail was a warning sign. James knew he had to get away from the evil he could feel and it was a sure sign that Morkann, their enemy was near. He turned to his brother.

"I know she is here! I can feel it; something has changed. I can smell her presence in the air. She is back!" James glanced all around him, his eyes wide open like a raccoon hunting in the dark. Petrified with fear, he felt a sudden urge to wander on and to leave the school grounds.

"This air is different, Tom. I can sense the vibrations. Something is wrong, and I know she is back. Tom, we have to get back to the other planets, and we have got to save Mom!"

Tom felt fear prickle his scalp like a thousand ants crawling over his skin. He was baffled by James, and the more he listened, the more he felt his skull begin to shrink as if it had been eaten by fear itself. He looked down at his hands, glaring at his palms. His hands were damp, and his mouth turned dry, his stomach twisted, and his throat clogged so tightly that he had to let out a stifled cough. He took in a gulp of air, trying to clear his lungs. Tom gazed at his older brother, his eyes devoid of any moisture and wide open, as big as lollipops.

"Look... look at that woman! SHE is staring at us". Her beauty silenced them both. Tom snapped at James noticing the strange woman draped in a blood fur red coat who just happened to appear at random along the corridor. At first, James thought it was a parent. Then as he walked past glancing at her sarcastic smirk, he paused for a moment, biting his lip, as he caught a fleeting glimpse at her while he walked past. It WAS her! He tried to stare her out, but each time he would try and return the stare she would simply vanish reappearing at a different part of the corridor.

"I think that was her! Morkann—in that blood red fur coat and silver hair! Crikey!

She is a chameleon!" James snapped. Uttering every word slowly in sheer horror, "Come on! We have got to get out of here!"

Having stopped running, James dipped his head trying to inhale deep gulps of air. He was huffing and puffing heavily to try to catch his breath. With a deep frown and supporting his legs, he turned to look at his angst-ridden brother.

The young men became nervous. They now knew Morkann was back and she wanted to cause their demise including their Mothers. Now the game plan had changed. Her motives were dark and she was able to transform into any creature or being when she wanted to obtain her way. Her wrath was near and without control.

Tom was astounded. He paused; his eyes shot open wild like a midnight owl. He realised what was going on, he turned to face his brother and both displayed deathly fear etched upon their faces. The young men began to scan the area in search of Morkann and her evil ghouls, although they would not be able to do anything even if they wanted to. However, she was a known chameleon, a warrior, and a malevolent creature who would not fear any terrestrial being, let alone a human carbonite. She was able to take any mask, emulate any voice, while slithering into an image she thought would gain her access to conduct her devilish deeds.

"James, well let's go back to the school, we know the route from there and it will be an easy way to get back those planets!" Tom suggested eagerly hoping they could go through the boiler room as they did before.

"Sure, could do Tom, but there is something we must do first and urgently. Come on; we have to get back to Mom quickly, she is in danger! Let's just see if she is OK first," suggested James as he quickened his pace.

"Yes, OK, you know we could go back through the boiler room?" replied Tom, still puzzled.

"Tom, I can feel her, I can sense it. She's here! She just brings doom, gloom, and malice. I could see her through her image, and I could feel her in the Earth! I saw her with my eyes, and I felt her presence. She is back, Tom!"

They were outside the college everything was still and appeared in a colorless shade. The drab concrete buildings looked as if there were made from old mottled brick, standing tall, proud, ridged, and cold as they glistened in the autumn-red sky. Although everything and everyone appeared as nothing had changed there was something not quite right about this day.

There was a constant buzz of cars zooming past on the roads, random horns tooting through the busy streets. People were rushing and walking with their heels clicking onto the grey concrete pavement, all just going about their daily businesses. However, something seemed unsettling. James could feel the whirling of air around him. He could hear the howling of wind and was able to see the trees gently swaying. He knew it was an omen that Morkann was in their presence. He frowned, creasing his eyebrows like a vulture off in search for its prey.

The obscure woman stood out from the crowd like a porcelain statue etched out of Michelangelo's marble collection. She gave a fixed gaze at James, her opaque pupils dilated, dazzling to try and hypnotize the boys.

Her red fur jacket was so lifelike. The strands appeared to be moving by themselves. The red tresses of her coat so vibrant in color it was difficult to judge whether indeed it was just a fur jacket or whether there were animals wrapped over her torso, about to pounce on anyone walking past. She was odd in appearance, with her silver hair cut to precision.

It was as if a mannequin had come to life. She was a picturesque figure of svelte beauty, no doubt, but she was too surreal.

As she glided through the walkway, James felt it like a shimmering shadow silently slipping into the crevices with a hidden secret. Maybe it was just her short, ghostly silver hair positioning itself like a perfect silhouette, with her tight black leather jeans clinging to her body like skin.

Her scrawny hands were covered with tight black gloves, even though it was not winter. James caught her staring at him with her slinky, light eyes, her deathly pale skin in her elaborate clothing made her stand out from the crowd. She was stared at him as he ran out of the college.

He stared back at her, their eyes locked but she quickly turned away and then disappeared amongst the crowd. He shook his head in disbelief. James contemplated whether the stony woman had anything to do with Morkann or indeed was it her in disguise.

Chapter II
The Medusa Illusion

James couldn't help but notice the lone, strange, beautiful woman clad in a short red fur jacket with swaying luscious velvet strands—each one like a live snake yet in deep slumber waiting for its call, as they ran for the exit.

Could it be her? Was it her? Was this Morkann in a new image? James was mesmerized. She had looked so different. The strange woman had just suddenly appeared outside the college entrance. The woman scrutinized the boys as they walked past watching and following them both.

The time was moving to five o'clock in the afternoon. His face appeared grief stricken as he became edgy and anxious. He began to remember the princess and Unicorn he had left behind on the planet after his last visit. He wondered if she would still be alive, along with the Unicorn he had nursed back to life.

Feeling uneasy he did not know where she would be. He turned to face his brother, biting his upper lip and still thinking about the woman they saw earlier, questioning Tom.

"Listen; did you see that woman, Tom when we were leaving wearing THAT coat? It WAS her; she is the one. She is! It's got to be—I felt it. Morkann is back!" James gazed deeply at his brother.

"That evil…! Why would she come back now? Why has she come back?" bellowed Tom. Tom grimaced and gave a fearful expression about the obscure slender woman, now believed to be Morkann, in the fiery red fur jacket and with wild silver hair. "Come on! We better go; you are right, James!"

There she stood, standing like a statue, at the college exit. She appeared to be waiting, but for who?

"Tom, did you see that woman?" James questioned anxiously.

"I did, crikey, it's her isn't it!" replied Tom.

"THAT woman…oh no! James!" snapped Tom. "What are we going to do?" He paused in horror. He could feel his blood rushing through his veins, creating a flushing glow of red on his arms and face. James knew they were now in terrible danger.

"I am convinced it was her too! She was just—I am sure it was her; it was her!" James bellowed. He paused, glancing around him, in a deep gulp of air. He concluded with a sniffle, "Tut...oh never mind...come on."

James dipped his head, perplexed at what he had seen, and with a screwed up face, he walked away. But he felt it was surely the demon princess Morkann. There were too many coincidences, as well as his premonition. James became irritated, as he knew it had to be Morkann, or something to do with her, since everything pointed toward her. James had a sure sense that the woman he saw had something to do with Morkann, for she was too different; and stood out. It was imperative that the demon Queen, Morkann had to be stopped in her quest to oust the boys and their Mother of their throne.

James and Tom just wanted to get back home to check on their Mom quickly so that they could all return to the planets.

They approached the main road, but the strange woman had vanished. James convinced himself that the obscure woman he saw was Morkann. He felt indisputably that she had come from the planet that they had visited. Along the road, the cars drove carelessly, hooting and tooting through the slippery network of roads, which was deafening, and many people frowned when the driver of one car would stop and partake in a heated conversation with the driver of another. The black asphalt shone like polished liquorice, with the traffic lights protruding proudly like buttons from a Lego set: red, orange, and green all flashing intermittently.

They decided to take the little blue hopper bus outside their college to go home, their pensive faces distraught with anxiety, for they were unsure whether this was the day that Morkann had returned to haunt the family, disguised as the woman with the silver hair and flame-red fur coat. The little bus pulled up, grinding to a stop, James jumped on, only to find the bus exploding with people standing and shoving due to the lack of space.

"Quick, jump on!" James instructed Tom impatiently as he scanned the bus in search for some empty seats.

When both boys were on the bus securely, all the passengers looked on as if they had never seen any empty seats before or indeed two young men. James and Tom were trying to negotiate their way through the over packed aisle, and wondered how any space would become available. After a short time they spotted some seats toward the back of the bus. James pulled his grey hessian rucksack high onto his shoulder as they began to walk through the aisle, wobbling along the gangway like astronauts marching in a gravitational abyss.

Then James spotted the two seats toward the back of the bus, but the aisle was heaving with people and shopping bags. They both very carefully to the only two remaining seats and sat down. Relieved, they placed their heavy rucksacks onto the floor.

The young men patiently waited for the bus to stop, gazing at the passengers around them who were just glaring back at the two of them, up and down, almost as if the two young men were escaped convicts.

James became fidgety and tried to break their glare. Frowning, he peered outside through the window—the short journey felt as long as forever—then he dipped his head, staring back at his hands. James raised his head to glance back at the passengers discreetly. But then he caught sight of the woman he had seen before, was it Morkann? He thought, but she was beautiful. He was close enough to see her face now, and she had a milky complexion that looked like porcelain, fragile and delicate, her light eyes sparkled, and her short, eerie, silver hair appeared to shimmer in the florescent light of the bus, swaying gently as the bus wobbled along the road. She wore the vibrant thick fur jacket that embraced her as if it were her own skin, yet the draping tresses appeared alive, like pumas prowling in a swampy rainforest. It was the woman he had seen outside the college. James continued to glare at her; something was not right. As he gawked, once more her beautiful face melted into a hologram of horror. This confirmed any doubt it was her!

The creature James witnessed was indeed Morkann the evil demon Princess who wanted to dominate with her dark powers and rid the mortal world of Lindiarna and her boys. James now had to warn his brother. His dreaded fear had become a reality. The journey should have been shorter, but for some reason it had dragged on like a bad dinner. James knew it was her. Morkann, with her short, sharp glances and smirks, confirmed to James enough of what he had to do.

The little bus merrily zoomed through the roads, swaying side to side in the short time before they were to reach their destination. Morkann had made her presence felt, and she knew James and Tom were from the McGuire household. They had become her targets.

Tom and James both rose from their seats to disembark, but James kept twisting around to catch glimpses of the strange woman—strange because she did not fit into the group of people seated on the bus. He was certain it was, Morkann and he now wanted Tom to see the facade behind the beautiful woman. He wanted to make sure Tom would see her too transformation into the slippery snakeskin, with her twisted mouth and demonic hollow eyes and Medusa hair, all reappearing as Morkann.

The young men shot up out of their seats to ring the bell for the bus to stop, and as they did the strange woman smirked wryly at James. She knew James had seen her real image through the facade, and she also realised that James was now fully aware that she was back. James grimaced and turned in anguish, trying to see her through the holographic image. He quickly sat back, sheepishly glaring intently at the hologram. Morkann had shape-shifted into an image of a beautiful woman once again, but James was able to see right through her, and the more he looked, the more he was able to see her real face behind the mask. Her mask would melt away intermittently, darting from one image to another, back and forth, back and forth at great speed. James turned his glare away quickly, not wanting to see her abhorrent images, until she, he hoped, would disappear. But it was HER, and she was not able to hide the truth of her malevolent self for long.

In all the commotion Tom was totally unaware of what was happening to his brother. He was blissfully unaware of what James was in view of and subjected to. He simply thought the strange woman was too beautiful to be Morkann and that it had been a complete coincidence that she was seated on the same bus heading in the same direction as they were.

The fiery red fur on her coat then began to move until it came alive. Her fur tresses started to convert into slippery brown and golden snakes, slowly lifting and sliding to wrap themselves around the woman as the creature came alive. Then they slowly displayed their evil, glaring green eyes that were able to transfix and hypnotize anyone in her path. The tresses from her coat began to lift gently and transform into a fiery red furnace of hell itself. Gazing, she laughed at James with a sniping, evil wail. Her neck now stretched to its fullest extent, while her coat still swayed like a snake before its charmer.

Each strand of fur swaying independently like abhorrent anaconda snakes, slithering, oscillating and hissing for their prey, their bulging eyes an iridescent emerald protruding a rage so abhorrent. Their long, slithering tongues slowly slid around the body of the coat and through each formed strand of the fur coat. James returned a frown, dipping his eyebrows in anguish, and then she released her voice: "The enemy is nearer than you think—mortal one!" She wailed and hissed, before tailing away.

He stared at her for a fleeting second. Then his glare became fixated in a hypnotic spell as he became trapped like a fly. She gave a cruel crafty smile that twisted at the edges of her thin evil mouth. Then suddenly she gripped his arm, allowing her devilish tresses of fur to wind and wrap and twist themselves around James's arms and waist. She had him, and like a Venus flytrap, she entangled him. Her Medusa tresses danced around his waist and arms as the faces of evil with sharp dagger teeth snapped and bit at him. Her malevolent image made sure that each strand of fur exposed, mutated into a dazzling group of eyes with tongues slithering and stretching out of their mouths, as if longing to take a bite out of James. The venomous serpent wriggled about, trying to get his first bite. The serpents were hungry, continually nipping at his torso. James was retching; his insides started writhing as though he'd just swallowed the live snakes themselves. He tried in vain to escape from Morkann's clasp, yet no one could hear him or even see him. He was now invisible to all. Morkann's cloud of invisibility had taken effect. No-one could see James or what was happening, but James was able to see through the cloud. It was like time had frozen.

Tom watching James was unable to see the horror of Morkann's transformation. In the horror which occurred James called out to his brother, but the snakes slid over his body enveloping him tightly.

The long thin multi colored snakes were sliding around him and gripping his waist tightly. James tried to push them away but was unable to.

He was petrified, perspiring heavily, and turning his lip down in distressed fear. Now, traumatized and stunned at Morkann's response and how the beautiful image that initially lured him toward her had transformed suddenly then gripped him. The bus was slowing down, but still the snakes gripped James and still no one could see the commotion of what was happening. All the passengers were busy looking out of the window as was an apprehensive Tom. However, he along with the other passengers had been placed under a subconscious trance, complete hypnosis, the invisibility cloud had worked and Morkann was able to dispel her malevolent warning of rage to James. They were all unable to view her devilish demeanor entrapping James. The passengers, including Tom appeared dazed, smiling chatting or just peering out of the window, whilst James was being attacked! No-one was able to even hear a sound of or see the venomous snakes, which had wrapped themselves around him or even hear him yelling. A demon visibility cloud had been thrown over the eyes and ears of all in the bus so that no-one was able to witness the occurrence. As soon as the bus slowed down and stopped, James pulled away from the last snake attached to him then shot out of the bus like a bullet fired from a gun.

"Come on! Now!" shouted James, encouraging Tom to quickly jump off the bus.

"Did you see what just happened?" asked James worriedly. He started brushing the remnants of the snake saliva from his sleeve. "Oh yuck—this is disgusting!"

"James, I couldn't do anything. I was frozen, but I DID see it! You OK?" he asked, completely in distress."

"YOU DID! Why didn't you do anything then? Did see her coat transformation? I knew it was her!"

"I couldn't! I was frozen out. Even if I wanted to I couldn't have she blocked any access I would have wanted...!" Tom protested. They walked closer to their home.

James was still in agony from his blood-soaked arm and waist, which Morkann had caused.

The two young men held their personal secret close, yet sometimes inadvertently their appearance spoke a thousand words.

Tom watched James in pain, "Do you want me to sort out those keys?" he said

"Yes! Oh my arm". James bellowed.

"Why couldn't you do anything again?" James said, still not convinced Tom was unable to do anything.

30

"James, are you okay? She did this?" he questioned trying to stem the flow of flowing red blood from his torso and shoulder.

"Why did you not do anything?" asked James.

"She's come back, Tom! I saw her face! She is the evil within the dark world; there is no doubt!" thundered James with his face full of anger.

Tom could see how distraught his brother had become.

"I tried to stretch out my hand to help you - but I couldn't see you, I was frozen!"

"You were not frozen Tom, she had blinded you with the invisibility cloud".

James thought exclusively about the events with the strange woman and how she took on a beautiful appearance. If she was Morkann, why did she let me go? He wondered she was the one who, like a shimmering shadow, appeared from nowhere yet slipped away, lurking into the crevices, only then to be seen on the journey home as a normal human, albeit a beautiful woman. It was the demonic flame fire fur coat—with the Medusa-like tresses flowing freely and how they suddenly metamorphosed into small slithering snakes that wrapped themselves around his arm and body and, with leering eyes and slithering tongues, stroked, grabbing and lunging at his body randomly—James had been hurt and was bleeding. He tried in vain to stop the flow of blood from his arm and waist, but he dropped to the ground. Tom came running to his aid.

Tom wiped his brow, and then paused horrified, in pain, gasping anxiously about what had happened and what was about to happen.

"Tom don't worry, come on we are home now".

He approached the front door in deep thought, fumbling with the metal front door keys he was holding. It was evident that the incident had affected him and it was a message he would convey to his Mother. His hands became swollen, red, and sore from the cold wind biting at his fingers. He positioned the keys to click into the lock, but they began to slip through his numb fingers as he tried painstakingly to unlock the front door that somehow appeared heavier and more cumbersome than usual. Clearly something that took normally just seconds was strangely taking longer. His hands, now felt like fish fingers taken out from the freezer. Tom walked around the front area of the house to check for any one following them. The sharp evening wind slapped at his hands, biting each fingertip as he tried desperately to click open the metal lock on the front door.

However, in his frustration, the keys became all tangled into a giant metallic puzzle. He continued working as quickly as he could, trying to hold onto the keys while shuffling through them looking for the right key, but the keys just all appeared the same. It had been a good few moments and James had exhausted every key as quickly as he could.

"Shall I try?" asked Tom watching James struggle.

"Go on, here", James reluctantly handed over the bunch of keys to his brother.

James glanced back swiftly, in the distress that Morkann's ghouls should suddenly appear, as they had a habit of popping up unexpectedly from nowhere with the ability to transform themselves into whatever was needed at that moment. It was a known fact that Morkann was darkness, full of complete malice, with malevolent actions. She was evil beyond evil, with various traits of a selfish mind. Her wish was to be the dominant queen of the galaxies to rule all beings and creatures. She would always appear as a menacing silhouette; not only that, but Morkann and her army of ghouls at odd times would scan the area, like wild hyenas on an African savannah searching for their prey.

They were ruthless. Morkann's ghouls would frequently appear, armed with blazing whips and demonic artillery such as long stakes with protruding, rotating serrated blades and spokes that could slice any flesh as their weaponry would rotate at speed upon a wheel. Occasionally they would use long swords, slashing and killing at random. They would gorge out the eyes of any being or creature, who would dare to look at them, or anyone who would try to stop them in their battle for their demon queen.

James knew, as did his brother, that the Morkannis or ghouls of Morkann could not and would not be casually destroyed; significant power was to be required. Perhaps, it was the power of his Mother and Jambalee, his Mother's loyal servant which would have to be called upon, for it was only them that would be able to defeat the dark dragons and ghouls once and for all. They rivaled the dragons' and ghouls' capacity for ferocity and destruction, bringing goodness and faith with hope, which the land had not yet seen. James knew that if this did not happen, their land could be obliterated for good. It was only a question of time as to when they would have to revisit the planets in order for peace between the outer galactic planets and creatures to ever be renewed.

Tom, having taken the keys continued fidgeting with them. James became more and more agitated, began Mumbling to himself of a plan to revisit the planets. Trying to hold back his frustration, James, who was now six feet tall and a handsome young man with a muscular figure; wavy black hair; and sharp, interesting, piercing blue eyes, looked back at his younger brother,

"Tom, tut we can't be here all day! Just sort out these keys—please!" James snapped.

James was deep in thought, and he was in pain, thinking about Morkann and the snakes biting and snapping at him. He knew he had to return to the land to finalise the dispute. How would they be able to get back to the Oblivionarna and Moradiya? The Redwood Coast Tree was no longer present, and Jambalee was no longer to be seen as before. He pondered on their imminent route of how they would be able to revisit the distant lands.

The secret, which was sacred and could not be shared or uttered, just in case Morkann's ghouls might hear or come to know of the fact their Mother was hiding in their midst, placed the family in extreme danger.

Out from the hazy evening, a steaming wine-colored mist in all the hollows silently crept through the air. It had roamed through the long road where dazzling blue sirens shrilled in the distance; it was like an evil spirit seeking rest and finding none. Tom watched in awe as to where the long wave of mist was headed. As it found its final resting place, Tom and James were sure the ghouls would now shoot out from within the clearing.

The wavy mist brushed against Tom's face, he blinked to let his eyes water. He was focused, holding the keys he walked around the house closer toward their intimidating dwelling, avoiding the branches from the old wild hedge, which lurked up at him at an angle trying to warn him away. Walking forward, not looking down, as he desperately wanted to get away from the now eerie side entrance. He eventually clicked opened the big pine door that stood proud conspicuously looking at him with its eye patterns carved into the wood, strung together like the thread from a needle.

Finally, Tom clicked the keys into the lock.

Once the door was finally open, both young men entered their home.

Tom walked into his house, and James slowly followed, still turning around quickly to look across the road in hope of seeing the colossal Redwood Coast Tree he had seen many years before. Tom handed the keys to James for safe keeping then he walked away into another room.

James felt a cold shiver run down his spine, and he dropped the keys onto the white wooden shelf in the hall and looked at Tom walking away. The house felt strange, yet this was his home. It did not feel normal; the home in which he grew up in and for a split second it felt empty, clinically empty, devoid of any love. The house was motionless and silent. James could only hear his footsteps on the wooden floor. Conversely, nothing appeared the same since that day—a day when his heart missed a beat. He knew in his heart that she was the one who captured it. For days and months, he reminisced about the rescue of Princess Anna-Lisa. She had stayed in the galaxy along with the Unicorn, he had nursed back to life; whilst James was unaware Morkann had imprisoned them both in her, demonic tower of death *Belle á Noir*. It had rained the night before, and mist was now creeping in. A soft blanket of cold purple steam swathed into the room, leaving a stony feeling as the brothers walked through the large, slightly sparse room.

James roamed throughout the house without direction. Everything was still. .He wandered aimlessly into every room, opening each door and peering curiously, searching for his Mother. James gazed everywhere, Morkann was here; he could sense it. For some strange reason, the house felt larger than usual, with the last room shrouded by a thick dark cloud of dust, enabling a bright light nova to reflect off intervening interstellar dust, there it was a light echo swiftly rotating. James, now aghast not knowing if he would be confronted by the devilish Morkann or her ghouls was relieved the door to the room had finally clicked open.

"James, did you find Mom, is she here?" asked an irritated Tom.

They both walked downstairs, their shoes knocking on the wooden floor. For some peculiar reason, James rushed back upstairs. He had to go back and revisit the room shrouded in the eerie mist. He walked inside, and around every corner of the room. There was a haze of unspoken promise and an aura of malicious intent. Tom continued searching for his Mom downstairs walking into each room, opening the doors. James was now convinced Morkann was back and her spirit was present. However, the silence in the house was haunting and unbroken. The wooden floors didn't hold any of the warmth of the once family home they all shared. Why would it? There had been much strife, and it was difficult to lead a normal life they once knew.

Then suddenly the phone rang—loudly. James didn't run to answer it; somehow he felt it odd that it should ring at this time. It never did before, so why did it have to ring now? He scowled while Tom watched his brother's reaction. Finally James ran downstairs hearing the telephone ring out. He reached gingerly for the phone.

"Hello?" he said tersely.

After a slight pause, a chilling voice echoed on the telephone line.

"You think you have got away. You think you have won. Ha-ha! Think again, child, you cannot run from me! Now there is only one way! I have waited many Earth days..." The voice broke off into a shrill scream before resuming.

"A deep darkness will fall. It will rip from you all that is good. You will not be able to sustain the penance of good!" The voice echoed in James's ear. "I will see you, and I will wait for your demise!" The raspy, eerie voice trailed off again into a wild, piercing cry, fading into nothingness, until the sound returned to the cold, frightening monotone of an empty phone line.

"Child. Death." I think I know who that was!" James stared out with an incredulous look, continuing to ask himself questions. "What does that mean? I know who that is! Urgh," he groaned. It was a eureka moment. James let out a long sigh of relief.

Retorting angrily, while holding and glaring down at the telephone line, he demanded a reply. But the voice had gone, all that remained was a monotonous dull tone.

James had become enraged at the mere suggestion that he should be called a child. His suspicion of Morkann, once again had been confirmed, so why was she teasing him? He became somewhat startled at the mention of death.

It was apparent that the wrath had reached a head. Morkann wanted a final resolution—which could only mean death. If it were Morkann, the Temperatia would certainly cause an angry storm, with many winds roaring into the horizon, causing hurricanes, volcano eruptions, flooding, and tsunamis. Of course it was inevitable that she would split the Mortal moon into three by covering the sun and the mortal land.

However, James knew who it was on the telephone calling to scatter their rage toward them. Tom peered wearily at him.

The phone rang again echoing through the hallway. Once the receiver was lifted the voice shrilled once more in an eerie tone. James, still holding the receiver, glanced around at the room in trepidation, noticing Tom peering wearily at him. Precipitously, the phone line once again sent out a dead, cold dragging tone. James held the handset away from his ears, trying to protect them from the trilling, monotonous tone. The eerie sound was very sharp and piercing, trying to drill through into his eardrums. Listen, she is talking again" James instructed frantically moving one arm up and down while the other held the handset.

His eyes were now fixated, and glaring hard, had become waterlogged. He licked his lips and glanced back at Tom who was now tense, with his furrowed brow and frown as his sweat began to gently cascade down his face into his eyes.

James, still holding the bold, red-handled receiver, recollected the creepy voice. All that remained on the other end of the receiver now was a still monotone chilling tenor.

The words still echoed through his head like a wild beast. What did it mean? He thought hard to himself and became puzzled with the conundrum. What does she want? Why is she scaring us all by appearing in her menacing specter?

"If this is Morkann, she is consumed with a deathly vengeance, James" said Lindiarna. Who walked in from the kitchen? "James, what happened to you?" She queried noticing his blood soaked torso. Totally confused and with a forlorn gaze, he slowly shook his head as if he were shaking his doubt away. What did it mean, 'Tonight we shall meet again'? James slowly recited each word of the call back to himself.

It was like a twist in the stomach that had taken hold of him. The hairs on the back of his neck shot out like barbed wire and his arms were suddenly covered in goose-bumps from the shock of hearing the raspy voice on the telephone, with the fright of how the strange, sound reverberated around the house, bouncing off each wall.

Then without warning—smash!—James was thrown back onto a chair like a rag doll from the sound of shattering glass like a bolt from the blue. His eyes waterlogged, but

James did not cry; he was too resilient. He could feel the urge to yell out his strong, suppressed emotion of anticipation of what was about to happen. His Mom was right, it was Morkann, who had spoken on the telephone! He felt any doubt was eradicated.

The room suddenly grew dark except for the orange streetlights that were streaming sharp rays of light in through the hallway window, casting long shadows across the wooden floor and glowing onto his face. Now filled with anxiety, James slammed the phone receiver down and ran straight into the kitchen, Tom quickly followed.

"Mom, come in here - please?" James shouted.

He became anxious, growing thirsty, he walked over to the fridge, yanked out a large carton of juice, and began to slurp at it. James then threw the carton down, spilling the liquid everywhere.

"Oh no!" James rubbed his brow, becoming frustrated and perplexed.

Unexpected footsteps filled the room and Lindiarna appeared in front of James, her eyes squinted and her lips tight and worried.

"Mom!" James stared intently at his Mother. "Do you know who called? You were right, you know who it was don't you? I saw her?" Tom listened intently at the strange telephone call between James and obscure caller,

"You think you would be able to rule the galaxy? Then think again! "Argh!" Morkann screamed. *Vos mos nunquam reign terra quod est mei!* she wailed and howled. "You will never rule this land; it is mine, only mine!"

The voice shrieked. "Of course, it would be very difficult for you if you were to have no life."

The voice then shrilled and faded away, leaving a deafening monotonous tone trailing on the phone. James, still holding the handset, took in a gulp of air and tried to relax his wide-open eyes. James, still holding the receiver, abruptly peered down on the red plastic handset, still reciting, and then began to slowly mime each word, trying to work out what the intent of this voiced message from the being or creature was. He recited each word slowly and dubiously as he turned to Tom and his Mother, puzzled and alarmed. Taking stock as to what had just occurred he frowned, peering at his brother, hoping Tom would suggest a solution to the increasing puzzle of the words the voice had left behind.

James was completely apprehensive of what he had seen and heard. Lindiarna did not say anything, instead, she appeared concerned, grimacing, peering at the spilt drink on the floor. She then walked out of the room along the wooden corridor.

Tom glanced at James and then watched his Mother walking away, reflecting on what she had said. She was out of the room contemplating her next move. Lindiarna was pensive, aware that if she returned to the planets before her time, she would face her demise. It was a risk that she would now have to face.

"James, Tom, are you two okay?" Lindiarna asked wearily

"Mom, I think we all have to go back, Tom bring the items – you know where they are?" James suggested defiantly.

Tom nodded, and walked into his room to locate the items.

James quickly turned to his Mother and then to Tom, his eyes as wide open as a nocturnal animal's.

Lindiarna faced her boys, knowing that if she left to return to the planets she would have to forfeit her life. She was petrified and yet needed to answer her boys—she was in a very precarious predicament.

She understood why she had been living in the mortal world and she understood the only way for her to be saved from Morkann was to remain on Earth, however she also knew it was now time for her to return to the land, otherwise all life on Oblivionarna would be enslaved. Lindiarna realised the implications of her return to the planet, and that she would have to forfeit her life.

James shrugged his shoulders in despair, not knowing the reason of his Mother's hesitation. He turned his elbows in while he pondered about the imminent return to the strange land.

Recollecting, James wondered, as he did on many occasions about the Unicorn he had rescued on that eventful day from the ditch of doom and the dark demon tower, Belle á Noir, where the princess, Anna-Lisa was imprisoned. Tom felt all James really wanted was to see the strange princess with her melodic voice and captivating charm again. It was Princess Anna-Lisa who seemed to have captured his heart.

James quickly reverted back to the telephone call, and turned to his brother, who was watching him carefully, with obscure facial expressions.

"Did you understand any of that" Tom asked

"Mmm…kind of, but I know it's HER, Morkann" answered a perceptive James.

"What did she mean though?" James mouthed back to Tom, referring to the telephone call. This was the first time James had said anything seriously to Tom after their tumultuous visit to the galaxy.

The war between Morkann and Lindiarna began many light years previously, when Lindiarna was a mere child and when the doors of death were forced open, and the war enraged. The two kings from the lands of Oblivionarna and Moradiya battled over ownership and rights for their creatures. It evolved into a dangerous place where lives where threatened. King Cepheus of Oblivionarna, sought refuge for his young daughter, Lindiarna, realising that she would be killed he sent her to Planet Earth to live amongst the mortals thus avoiding the perils of the demon King Polydectes together with his daughter Morkann. Ever since then Lindiarna discovered life living amounts the mortals on Earth. Morkann had vowed to take her vengeance on Lindiarna.

Tom frowning peered toward James,

"I don't know, but whatever was said, I think you're right; it's Morkann—the Temperatia—the Manipulator of Storm Winds. She is our enemy, James, our enemy—Morkann! She will want the power to enslave us all and Oblivionarna and eventually the carbon world! We have to stop her" Lindiarna bellowed with worry.

Tom's eyes opened brightly, and he remained wide-eyed as he shook with dread. He could now feel Morkann's presence, and her wrath seemed darker than ever before.

James faced his brother, who appeared cautious, scanning his surroundings worried that Morkann or her devilish ghouls would suddenly appear, without warning. He could feel James's anger had diminished, all he could now think of was his family and keeping safe.

"Tom, we know she is back—right, so we have to take those items which Jambalee gave you. He and Tom began to analyise the raspy message. After much trepidation, the full meaning of the message became clear. They had cracked it. Both brothers began to work out what the conversation referred to.

James became angry. Why was it that she wanted him and his family dead? He continued to analyze each word, breaking each one down to a syllable, and as he did so, he became mystified and confused. He held his head in his hands pensively. His eyes were wide open, like a hooting owl's, searching, looking, and pondering about his quest.

"Yes, James it was her," Lindiarna replied. She calmly walked toward him. She realised Morkann was now after her boys too. The quest had grown and had become more volatile and dangerous; lives were now at stake.

"James, Tom, you two—you're OK, right?" She quickly looked over both her sons. Lindiarna's eyes were now darting from one son to the other at speed.

She took in a deep breath, as she knew only too well that this time the game she was playing had changed course, for now Morkann wanted more than just to avenge the war of Typhoona—she wanted to kill and eradicate everyone in her path. The fear of impending death was etched upon their tired, gaunt faces.

"I know who called, and I know why she has taken her time. But now she is back." Distressed, and with a forlorn face, Lindiarna felt she was in grave danger, perhaps more than ever.

Completing her powers and pondering over which of them would work, she lifted her head and peered out of the window. "Gosh...This Carbon world!" she lamented.

Tom, although a strong sixteen-year-old boy, threw his arms onto his Mother's shoulders, relieved she survived this long, despite the dangers she had faced. She was pleased that both her boys, now young men had returned home alive from each visit and that they were well. Now they were safe, and she knew that for each day that passed, it was a benediction from the mortal world. It had felt like that for

46

the past few years when James and Tom had returned from there deadly encounter with Morkann and also from the battle which had taken place earlier today.

When the boys crossed Morkann path in Moradiya it was ferocious, with both young teenagers witnessing death and hearing the pitiful cries and groans of pain. Of course, they had never seen such endless suffering when crossing the muddy crater in search of the princess. James, witnessing the Unicorns in pain, alone in a dark rift from a broken gorge, felt their anguish and needed to rescue at least one of them. Xleha, the Mercury king, malevolent friend of Morkann was soon met. It was him, the evil one who controlled the silver mercury acid liquid, which held the fire burning fiercely around the liquid. The furious furnace blazed as it roared, and yet still intrepid Xleha stood proudly among the flames, his markings on his strong, fierce frame shimmering against the roaring, incandescent blaze. James was brave; he stood in the melted mercury, and after much consternation, plunged into the liquid as small silver shards reflected his life in minute, broken pieces.

These, sharp glistening fragments were all scattered across the thick fluid. In that moment his life would never be the same. His eyes swept the liquid stream, trying to piece together the broken fragments of his life. Tom of course abstained from the liquid. He was only able to watch in agony after he suggested that it was not going to be helpful to enter the mercury liquid, as he felt it was too dangerous.

It was from that day that James comprehended the extent of the battle and the evil powers which controlled the planets through Morkann and her ghouls.

The brothers understood that the more tyranny occurring with the outer galactic planets, the more destruction would occur on Earth. Lindiarna quickly walked over to one of the lounge sofas, leading Tom by his hand, and sat down with him. She took in a deep breath, sucked in her cheeks for a split second, and with staring green eyes and dilated pupils, she glared intently at both her strong young sons. She had quickly realized that Morkann had shown her presence already. Turning to an apprehensive Tom, Lindiarna held his hand tightly and protectively, stroking with a woeful gaze as she watched his every move. Again she took in a deep gulp of long-awaited air and then turned sharply to face her older son, James.

"James, you do know that this mission is going to be very difficult and dangerous..." Lindiarna paused, having released Tom's hand she placed her arm on Tom's shoulder. She frowned, glancing at her humble, strong sons, James was restless. Lindiarna wondered apprehensively if she was making the right decision to tell him of her anguish. She let go of holding Tom's shoulder and smiled lovingly at him. Glancing back at James, she knew she would have to tell him of the story behind Princess Anna-Lisa and of course Morkann or better known as—Temperantia the Manipulator of Storm Gale—she was their enemy Morkann, who was born to cause havoc and destruction.

"James...I don't know if now is the right time, but then when is ever the right time? I have to say this..." She reasoned with her turmoil and bit her lips nervously and then gazed back at her older son.

"OK, I know you want to rescue and bring back the Unicorn and princess Anna-Lisa" She peered intently toward him, watching his every move. James, a charismatic, bold, eighteen-year-old young man with strong, high cheek bones and sharp, dazzling blue eyes, was every part human without a doubt. He stood casually turned to his Mom and replied to,

"Well, yes, I do. She is something strange, something quite unusual..."

"Yes, James, what I want to say to you is this: I don't think it's wise that you continue your friendship with Princess Anna-Lisa... not yet, the time is not right. Morkann must be curtailed in her vengeance first – You understand don't you?." Lindiarna was firm as she stared directly into her son's now lost, wide, sad blue eyes.

"Mom, right now the way I see it, is that we are going to have to leave and rescue who we can – right Tom." At that point Tom, who was listening intently and watching his Mother speaking to James, became startled. He turned sharply to face his brother.

Lindiarna smiled reassuringly,

"James, I know you want to help, but the battle ahead will be hard – you understand?"

James, now deep in thought, quickly looked to face his Mother.

"I know" I will be fine."

"Just make sure you have the weaponry with you and use it if you have to – Morkann is dangerous and destructive. When you rescue and get hold of Princess Anna-Lisa, think twice before you bring her back to Earth – James. Please"

"What do you mean?" he questioned, trying to get his Mother to tell him more. James angrily retorted, "I saved her from Morkann's clutches and took her away from that evil tower! I know she will to be better here, you survived here!—I know she will be safe here! She was so miserable, Mom, caged up in that dungeon tower; what was it called-*Belle á Noir?*" James paused, reflecting back to his moment of rescue.

"Oh yes, Belle-á-Noir. Mom, I just feel she and the Unicorn are in danger again. If they are still alive that is? She is in danger, real danger. I mean, I just left them there! You know that! I left her with the Unicorn and Jambalee!"

"She needs our help Mom!" He looked at Lindiarna in angst, hoping she would tell him to go and rescue her.

"We have to get her out of there, and away from that place!"

James was adamant and knew what he wanted. There was no one who was going to stop him or even reason with him at that very moment.

Holding his shoulder, Lindiarna peered intently into his deep blue eyes.

"James, if your love is strong and real, then you will win your battle, but remember: let bravery be your choice, not bravado." She smiled reassuringly.

"You are a handsome young man, James. I don't want anything to happen to you—either of you," she whispered, glancing over to Tom.

"Why don't you ever want to go back to that world, Mom?" James boldly retorted.

"James, some things don't' need to be unraveled".

Lindiarna locked her lips tightly and dipped her eyes not wanting to disclose the details of her life to her mortal sons, but she always knew one day that one of her boys would ask her about her planet.

She frowned, scrutinizing her sons, and she then closed her eyes. She took a deep breath, realising that it would be very difficult for her to confront both her sons with the truth as to why it would be hard for her to return to her original galaxy of Oblivionarna and that the same would apply to Princess Anna-Lisa, if she too were to be rescued and then to reside on Earth as a mortal/Carbonite. Lindiarna knew she would just have to blurt out her reasons for being so guarded.

She immersed herself once again in deep thought, reminiscing about her younger life, how she would witness the joys and colors of soft marble of the Palace of Greatness in the cosmic planet of Oblivionarna with King Cepheus and her loyal servant Jambalee.

It was King Cepheus who would guard her with his life, protecting her every move from the venomous King Polydectes and the avenging Morkann. Lindiarna had begun to realise from a young age that Morkann was extremely jealous and envious from her pursuits. However, her anger was venomous even when Morkann was young.

This may also have stemmed from the ferocious battle between the two planets, which had occurred sometime before. Since that time when nothing stood still, it was noted that the kings from Moradiya and Oblivionarna had become bitter rivals with no sign of reconciliation. Lindiarna's face changed suddenly; it seemed as if the color of danger smothered her eyes, wide open and bloodshot, glaring toward her son James. She knew the time had arrived for her to return back to the land she was forced to leave.

Lindiarna walked over to the window and looked closely at the green outside, searching the yard intently to find the Old Redwood Coast Tree. But it had disappeared. Lindiarna was aware of Hakeem and of his power of good. He had not reappeared to assist them in their new quest to leave the carbon world.

At that very moment, she turned quickly to face her boys. Her eyes bewildered, like a gazelle searching for safety as she realised that there was no hiding or concealing her power. She now was in a predicament to visit the land she had forcibly left behind and face her imminent demise. Lindiarna began to comprehend that they would all now travel together. She was anxious, intimidated of what would be before her, the unknown and the unchallenged, for time had passed, and she was no longer the creature she once was. Lindiarna had almost forgotten how to use her powers, as she never displayed her true identity or image of the princess which landed on earth on that solemn winter's night.

"Do you know what you will see?" Lindiarna questioned, anxiously. "My land, the land of Oblivionarna is good, but we will have to go to Moradiya the land of Temperatia, Morkann's land of doom and gloom."

Tom grimaced. "I have been there, but surely Jambalee will come to our aid, won't he?"

James glanced over at Tom, interrupting his plan.

"Yes, what about Halaconia? She will be there too, right?" Both boys then looked to their Mother for reassurance.

Lindiarna stroked her head wearily and pensively spoke to her boys. "No, they may not be! The land of Moradiya is not a good place; you've both seen it for yourselves. The Crater of Death is to be found hidden in the Valleys of Comets!"

"... And, what about Hakeem? He was the giant alien in the Gregorian robe who took us there? Will he be there?" James asked excitedly.

Turning to Tom, he hoped he would cut in and back him up with his suggestion.

"I mean, where would we find him? Everyone is scared of him!"

"Are we going to be alone then?" asked James.

Lindiarna spoke with a dejected gaze, peering at Tom.

"James, you are the strong one. We are going to find the Unicorn and Princess Anna-Lisa and I will regain my throne, if that's what you boys want? Whatever happens, we have to get to stop the constant incantation of death by King Polydectes and Morkann. It has to stop! The years of rivalry and hatred have to stop! For years I have carried this heavy burden of living in someone else's shadow!"

Lindiarna's voice developed into a loud, strong tone; she was determined like never before. Beaming like a full moon, she gazed intently at both her boys. The Carbonites were her children, although they were now grown up and had become young men. But would they survive?

Lindiarna was always anxious around James after he had returned from his last visit, having rescued the Unicorn from certain death and fallen for Princess Anna-Lisa. She knew only too well the type of calamities he would have been subjected to.

Lindiarna and her younger son Tom had watched how James had become quiet and reserved; maybe this was just part of growing up; who was to know? Or just maybe this was his mechanism of dealing with the many issues he now was subjected to.

The plan was set; they would venture into the galaxy planet once they had a date and their magic items with them.

The next day although the two young men were anxious and agitated, they decided to head for their old school, identifying it as a sure way to get back into the galaxy, and Tom knew the way. However, it had been a long time since Tom had used the route to access the planets; he was unsure he would be able to recall the route. He knew it was important, as he tormented over each step, he tried to remember the access point. Then it suddenly came to him like a bolt of lightning: "Eureka! I know how to get there!" He jumped at James in excitement.

It was all planned, and the family became anxious. "Right, you better take what you need," instructed Lindiarna. It was dark, and Tom began to gather his weaponry from his room, meticulously climbing up on the stepladder to reach the stored shield, sword and magic powder pot, which Jambalee had given him. They had all been hidden so trying to reach above the tall wooden wardrobe, holding on with his hands, hanging precariously with his nails on the wooden doorframe. On climbing up to reach each item, he carefully pivoted from the wooden ledge of the frame while he maneuvered his magic pot into his rucksack, tucking it in securely. He quickly then jumped down and began to search for all the other items he had hidden.

"Come on, Tom. Hurry up!" moaned James

"I think I have everything". What about Mom?" asked a worried Tom?

"She is going to have to come with us right." James glanced up at his Mother, who was watching close by. Lindiarna, knowing her fate on her return to the land that she had left behind, was determined to face the risk. She was tormented and in anguish. Her fear was etched upon her gaunt face and knowing her demise.

"Ok, I got everything now, come on," Tom said.

They all watchfully made their way to the old school, walking together over the old iron bridge, which suddenly just dipped into an opening, where the large wooden doors lead into the schoolyard. The light had turned gray, and everything around them seemed to hide in the shadows, with streams of yellow and white light sneaking through from the classroom lights, creating obscure monster shapes around them. James became tense, his mind buzzing with so many thoughts and questions that he would have to answer. James was worried and felt nervous, hoping Tom would remember the passage back into the planets.

Tom then whispered, "Follow me; come on." They all headed for the boiler room, their eyes floating like candles searching for a light. Tom gazed around him; it seemed very little had changed. The pipes were still metallic and colossal mapping the ceiling. After much deliberation and discussion, Tom glanced up into the darkness, wondering if he would be able to remember the route he took to discover the planet.

Then suddenly, in front of them, they saw a towering, svelte female figure appear. She was carved out the shadows. Her long, thick, luscious hair wrapped around her shoulders, draping almost to the ground, with splinters of golden light shining through and reflecting her sunlight-colored hair. Her body was adorned by a long white robe, while her thick hair stopped just short of touching the ground.

As the light flickered from the orange street lamps sneaking through the small windows, the sublime figure elevated forward. The flickers of light began to dance on the figure's golden hair, the essences of summer, a goddess of the sun causing soft silky strands to fall across her face like a siren leading everyone to sudden happiness. It was a cat-wheel firework wildly whirling and whizzing at great speed. The light caught some of her face and slid past her eyes, displaying her eternal beauty.

Her light eyes sparkled like amethysts, cut and sharp glistening in the prism of light. James felt as if righteousness itself had arrived to help them. He was completely mesmerized by the figure in front of them.

She then gently spoke, her voice echoing off the metallic maze of pipes. "Sons of Oblivionarna, I am here to guide you through to the planets. You are the worthy and righteous ones, James and Tom. We have been waiting for you."

Tom froze in trepidation. "Please, who are you?" he questioned eagerly. James stared at the obscure beautiful figure, watching her every move.

"I am Natalya. I am the embodiment of good. I am the love that you have. I am here for you, and I have come to help; remember; only righteousness will succeed. I am here to take you to reclaim your throne, so that goodness will prevail."

Her voice gently trailed off to leave a haunting echo rumbling through the metallic pipes. Natalya elevated toward the boiler room door, her light robe dragging across the floor. Lindiarna followed, equating each step to her life and reflecting back to her childhood in the Gardens of Lost Treasures within the palatial opulence of the grounds of Prytaneum. She was anxious and apprehensive of the impending encounters she was expecting to endure. Her torment was now etched upon her face after such a long time, but she knew it was inevitable and would end soon.

Tom looked up at James quickly, trying to recollect the initial route he had taken so long ago; his eyes opened wide, as if his eyeballs were trying to escape from their sockets.

Natalya gave a half smile, as her vibrant golden hair cascaded to fall onto one side of her tall, slender body. "Do you remember your route, Tom?" she asked with a forlorn gaze, goading him toward the entrance, now clear from any large clutter that there once was.

"Yes, it is somewhere here. I met the janitor last time but I know it is somewhere…"

Tom took a tentative step forward, gliding his hands about the space in search of the entrance door. While sliding his palms along the wall, he touched the cold, battered, old door hinged up against the wall in the far corner. Tom's heart raced, pounding like an elephant stampede, at his excitement of finding the entrance route.

"This is it!" he yelled out, frantically pulling the last few boxes away from the door. James began to help him hurriedly. "Oh this is it, this it!" He repeated in jubilation.

Lindiarna watched carefully and nervous, her eyes open wide and her heart jumping like a thousand gazelles.

Once all the various items of boxes and clutter had finally been pulled away, the entrance door became visible. There, it was, finally—the tattered, crumbling door stood proud and old. It was flaking, tatty and covered with dry peeling white paint. It seemed as if someone had tried to cover up the cracks and old rust from the decaying iron door with paint.

Tom was jubilant; he knew this was the door leading to the entrance of the other worlds beyond. He became excited, anxious of what was to confront him and his brother when they would finally enter.

James took in a deep breath and released it, puffing out into his cheeks like a hot balloon. The entrance to the intergalactic planets had been found it was now for real—no more searching for the planets beyond. They had located the door. James continued watching Tom's incredulous look.

His fear now changed into thoughts of him meeting his friends and his beloved Unicorn. The Unicorn, which he had left behind in the galaxy, became paramount. Anxious and bewildered, James turned to his Mother, whose eyes filled with moisture as she shed a lone tear. Smiling, Lindiarna turned to face Natalya, who knew of the tragedy which was to befall upon the family. She glared intently at the entrance to the worlds, and with her long slender arm stretching out she raised her hand for her delicate sleeve to droop. Then she pointed with her slim finger toward the door. Unexpectedly, a strange bright golden light appeared as she pointed to illuminate the obscure access route. It was like Pandora's Box had been found and was now ready to be opened. Tom glanced up at Natalya's finger, following the bright light source through to the door. He lunged forward and began tugging at the crumbling edges of the old iron door. Chipped white paint fell off in large clumps with a light noise, echoing on the maze of pipes hoisted in the air. Tom continued to heave and pull at the door with all his might until the door was slightly ajar, and in the process, more and more flaking paint fell off. James, who was much stronger, jumped in to help his brother. He pulled and tugged at the door until the gap became large enough for Tom to squeeze through. After one last tug, and the door flew open, throwing James and Tom backward onto the floor.

Then, small fingers of dim purple light began to seep through the crevice, lighting up the pathway indicating it was clear to walk into the entrance. Natalya gave an encouraging smile. The first test had been completed. The entrance to the galaxy was now visible. James felt although it was a dark chasm, had it not been for the fragments of purple light dribbling through the entrance it would not have been accessed.

"Urgh, that's it! You found it, Tom! You're in, Tom; good luck!" James said calmingly nodding to confirm to his brother before Tom vanished through the door his shadow disintegrating as he took each step.

Tom turned reassuringly to his brother and his Mother, whilst Natalya levitated like a celestial goddess, smiling to herself in recognition that Tom had entered the land alone, and the mission had begun. As Tom entered through the door, he cautiously nodded to confirm his departure to his family, hoping they would follow soon. He began to wander through the strange land, enticed by the buttons of purple light seeping through as a pathway light. Lindiarna pensively looked on, knowing she too would be joining her sons in the world she had once left behind. Natalya had completed one of her tasks. The brothers had reached the entrance point of the land of Oblivionarna. Tom had gone through dark tunnel and into the planet first.

It was only James and Lindiarna remaining for Natalya to complete her mission. Natalya then led Lindiarna through the small door as James watched, walking in haste into the planet. Lindiarna cautiously took each step and carefully, gazed all around her surroundings.

Tom wandered aimlessly into the dark, dense terrain through the comet-strewn land, each step creating a path of soft gravel footprints between the purple broken light drops from the surrounding area. As Tom pensively wandered through, his breath began to echo all around him, waning into an eerie silence. He found himself in a void space, an abyss, but he entered deeper and deeper into the land of the unknown.

The light source disappeared until nothing was seen and fell into darkness, everything became still. Reflecting on his last visit, his mind darted from one thought to another.

"Oh, I wish Jambalee was here, he would know what to do and where to go" Tom muttered to himself. Jambalee was Lindiarna's loyal servant. As he recalled, he shuddered at the very thought of the monster dragon Typhoeusina reappearing from his very first visit. Tom continued wandering through the barren terrain, vigilantly hoping not to trip over some of wild broken comets and stars strewn on the gritty terrain. He longed to see Jambalee, just to be reassured.

As he wandered deeper, into the planet it seemed to open up a kaleidoscope of colors with a wild array of rotating asteroids firing off into sporadic shots of cosmic fireballs. Natalya beckoned James, who now was starry-eyed watching Tom disappear through the boiler door, and as he did so, he became almost hypnotized.

Natalya gazed intently, watching every step Tom took, in the hope that the dragon monster, Typhoeusina, would not awake and cause havoc. Once again, Natalya decided to follow James and Lindiarna on their entrance. Both James and his Mom were terrified of approaching the unknown lands.

Natalya, sensing they were both extremely anxious, gazed at them. Her picturesque porcelain face hovered toward them closely as she uttered,

"The quest you fear to enter holds the treasure you seek." The family gawked up at Natalya before she spoke again. "King Cepheus was a noble king, and we, the people of Oblivionarna, admired him in his reign. You, Lindiarna, are bestowed to continue his legacy." Natalya spoke tersely, watching Lindiarna, and then stared pitifully at her. Natalya's amethyst eyes became bright, catching glimmers of a flickering light from the flying comets bouncing into the darkness from the galaxy.

"Morkann has cleared the path way so as to attack you! "There is no turning back; all the evil within her has driven her to insanity. She can no longer see right from wrong. She has rid our lands of anything good." Natalya said glancing at Lindiarna, and staring back at James's grief-stricken face, she frowned, took in a gulp of oxygen, and again tried to pacify Lindiarna.

"You must listen to me carefully. Oblivionarna represented the righteous, and you are the last jewel she needs to exterminate. She will do anything, with no remorse. She has killed your father and your Mother—your court has been cleared. You are now the only lapis lazuli left! She will trick you and change into anything her heart needs. She is able to just destroy your legacy. She will torment you until you give in to her requests. Even her thorns are toxic to the eye! Lindiarna, know this: she and her ghouls will be your demise. She will destroy anything in her way, even the thorn, to claim her victory alone."

As Natalya said each sentence, Lindiarna's eyes welled up with tears. James looked on with a sullen face. It was hard to see his Mother alarmed, yet still he did not understand why Morkann had so much hatred.

"Fear not, child; the fear she is trying to bestow upon you will not flourish. It cannot. Only righteousness will succeed! But each time there is a war in our lands, Temperatia will rule over the mortal world, causing much destruction and catastrophic death, and countless floods and many storms will befall your planet. She has the power to make mortal raise war against mortal, thus creating an apocalypse of hatred among Carbonites. You Lindiarna can change this forever, if you are willing to wage war against the demon queen Morkann, who you know in this life is Temperatia. Stop Temperatia and her wrath of hatred and evil from spilling into the galaxies!" Natalya spoke with such conviction peering directly into Lindiarna's eyes.

Lindiarna, nodding gently, confirmed her acknowledgment of the legacy left for her to continue, "Should anything happen, you will—", she said to James half-reluctantly. Lindiarna stopped suddenly overwhelmed by anguish and took a deep breath, braced herself and continued. "James, you are heir and shall be King of Oblivionarna". Lindiarna was adamant that James should be aware of the imminent quest.

"You must seek out the mirrors, and any small shards reflecting your life, which you must piece together to transform into your path. This will be your path, your way forward to succeed, on your quest. You must never give up, my brave son," she said, holding his strong arm with affection as she gazed deeply into his eyes.

Chapter III
The Wrath

(This chapter contains Latin)
Temperatia the Manipulator of Storm Force——the enemy——Morkann Tempestates
becon fortis — (Latin)

Knowing that the prophecy would shortly unravel, Lindiarna was both distraught and fearful. The poignancy of her predicament had etched itself in the shape of a disenchanted frown. She had endured mortality on planet Earth and it could not be in vain. Now two young brothers in their prime were the positive life force destined to restore rebalance. Morkann could no longer rule with such ferocious wrath——it had to come to an end. Change was inevitable. The question was, when would this change happen?

Lindiarna feared for the lives of her sons. She realized that Tom and James could never even contemplate living with ease on the planets that she had left behind. With a deep sigh, Lindiarna smiled courageously. Raising her inner strength, she turned to her sons and spoke gingerly. "We have a journey that we are going to do together. I must tell you this. It is going to be difficult for me... I never wanted you to see the real visions from the planets. You do realize this? Your faith in this land must not leave your soul. Everything you see has its roots in the unseen world; the forms may change, but the essence remains the same." The boys acknowledged her words with a nod, but knew the true meaning was yet to reveal itself.

Natalya continued to watch in silence, with the knowledge of what was to unfold including Lindiarna's fate. She held the secrets close to her heart but was unable to utter a single word. Natalya knew in her mind the horrors that would be and that only James and his brother would be able to do anything to avoid them. She was now lost in thought. Her mind was darting around all the activity that was yet to materialize. Natalya had the power to assist but was unable to. She turned to face Lindiarna. Lindiarna gazed into Natalya's amethyst eyes, which shone as bright as sparkling jewels set in a golden crown. Through her mystical eyes, Lindiarna became startled at her warning of the dangers that lay ahead. She turned and glanced around at the terrain that now appeared strange and perilous to her. As she did, Natalya spoke.

"Listen carefully to what I say, a veil of death with vile aspirations, with her large abhorrent beasts parading the tor of Moradiya, will greet you. Do not be perturbed by this greeting. Morkann will be lurking in the shadows of darkness. It has been written many years ago, when the world was young and the crater of death was formed, Morkann took power from her father, King Polydectes. So it was written that if you, Lindiarna, did not yield in Morkann's service, then your demise would be in your own life source. Just be aware, there will be creatures and wild beings from another world, accustomed to being hunted." Natalya was interrupted by an eager Tom, "But tell me your greatness, will we see these creatures?" he asked excitedly. "Yes, it is written!" she replied with great conviction. "But only if you manage to cross the Volcano of Doom in Moradiya,"

"Volcano of Doom!" The boys both said in unison, "Don't worry", Lindiarna said reassuringly. "I will be there too, and don't forget we have the weapons". "Urgh…I am not sure about this anymore. James, what do you think?" Trepidation had caught up with Tom albeit momentarily. James offered some consolation. "Tom, pull yourself together, we have seen worse! Don't forget the deadly Basilisk dragon!"

"Oh yes, if looks could kill, this serpent could turn a man to stone by its gaze alone!" Tom retorted, referring to the serpent, which had crossed their path previously.

Natalya peered closely at James and Tom before continuing,

The boys were stunned in horror, shuddering at the thought of Morkann's evil intent.

James did not know what to say, he felt as if he had been punched. Feeling a sudden dread Natalya, hovered toward the brothers,

"You will not be in slumber and you will witness dark worlds, and dark thoughts and how a dark demon queen now will reign your path. "Her chameleon tactics will send spine-chilling tremors through your bones," warned Natalya.

They did not fully comprehend the story behind the rage and wrath of the demon Morkann. The shield of life, which Jambalee had given to Tom in his initial meeting, was tucked safely in his grey rucksack and the bag opened the shield glistened across the sky, forming a rainbow of constellations of fire across the Milky-Way.

"These evil creatures of darkness lurk behind our thought memories. They have the power to transform their bad deeds into a good deed, but they will not. They will hinder any goodness that succeeds. Morkann vowed many moons ago that she would stop me in every step I would take or every veil or shroud that I should hide behind. She would destroy me—this was her vow!" Lindiarna said.

"James, you are a strong mortal, YOU must reclaim your right," Natalya insisted.

Tom listened intently before James interrupted, asking,

"I need to know, Mom, why is there so much hatred? Why does she show such malice" James was naïve and still trying to understand the wrath behind the malevolent creature Morkann.

"Yes, she is consumed with power. Her evil must be contained! There is no evil that cannot be stopped, for goodness must always prevail!" his Mother replied.

Tom tried to interrupt into the conversation, which was now near impossible, so he just watched and listened attentively.

"We have to stop the demon Morkann I will bring the potion pot!

He stopped suddenly as all the family and Natalya turned sharply to face him. "Well, I could bring the shield of life too," Lindiarna said.

"Good idea". James shouted.

"I am just as scared as you are too…"

"Well we all ARE! Tom, James, come on don't let her evil make us weak, we have a job to do, come on let's go!" Lindiarna ordered.

Lindiarna, still trying to compose her strength in front of her sons, smiled nervously and peered up at them.

"Her wrath is not without purpose, her envy is green and deeply rooted. She just wants the power to rule— simple. Her wrath, malice, and rage have never diminished." Lindiarna's voice began to fade, tailing off toward the end of her sentence.

Lindiarna was contemplative and had become very anxious of her impeding return journey as she considered the hazardous and arduous journey before them. How would she be able to guide her sons in a world that she had forgotten? She began to understand the enormity of her visit back to the planet. She would have to relinquish all her powers and indeed her appearance as a carbonite. As it began to dawn on her, the realization of her ever increasing demise became closer and she became silent, locking eyes with Natalya gave her a sense that all would be well. She reminisced of all the good times and the events that had happened during her Earth life. However, it was something that could not be sustained; this was inevitable. Deep in thought, Lindiarna was apprehensive of meeting the evil creatures and beings she had once left behind in the land of Moradiya.

Night fell into an abyss, with the eerie land disappearing into a tranquil, crisp silence. The stars shone brightly, red, copper, and florescent green twinkling high up in the Milky-Way, no one could have been mistaken for thinking that Jupiter and Mercury were dancing in the nebulas above amongst the bright Solar flares. It was the raging heartbeat of a hundred planets all trying to warn each other of Lindiarna's return. They were all illuminating in swaying in a zephyr and a gentle haze of purple velvet darkness.

Lindiarna was now pensive, her eyes hardened, like flashbulbs, snapped open and quickly staring out into the horizon, rapidly realising that the time had arrived to visit the land. This time Lindiarna had no say, she would have to go to try and break the pattern of death. Her thoughts, were in turmoil as they danced inside her head.

Gradually, a soft, orange, wispy cloud mist lifted, and in doing so, dull patches of a red vibrant glow glided far beyond the horizon, appearing like rising cliffs adorning the skyline. There they could see the active, red mountainous rocks now standing prominently. The comets thrusting spires of naked jagged spikes into the Milky-Way so high that it could be believed the very sky was perforated.

A sparkly tear tumbled down Lindiarna's soft face; the truth of her residing on Earth was now going to be made final. James looked at his Mother, Lindiarna and not knowing what else to do, he slowly placed his arm around his beloved Mother, sensing she was frightened of the arduous journey ahead. "Tom, come on. Get your weapons; we're going to need them!" James said, looking at that luminous red delight of the sunken sky above. "Look!"

The morning clouds had all but disappeared, stretching out of slumber, they began to take the form of a word, and begging to be read, NO! The inscription was visible using the strange, stringy clouds were trying to pass a message. The dovelike fluffy clouds were conveying a message and appeared in the shape of outstretched arms symbolically waving as if to warn the family not to go forward. Shrouded in a dark angry cloud, a red mist pointed to the eerie-looking clouds in front of them, where a haze of brilliant lights melted into the horizon. Both Tom and James took hold of their body

armor as quick as they could, for they realised their path was to be hazardous. The closer they paced toward the red eerie mist, vigilantly turning left and right, witnessing the many broken rifts and gorges as they would pass the mist it seemed to imprison them and enveloped them completely, trapping them into a void they would not be able to escape from. The red mist mysteriously then riddled around the land before it totally trailed away. They could see the mist like a snake coiling its muscular rings, catching the shimmering from the comets and broken stars that caught the light like prisms. Being led by a careful Lindiarna, the boys trekked slowly toward the black mountain that held the Tower of Belle á Noir, in the far distance. They gathered pace as they marched on cautiously over the precarious boulders and fallen star debris; they could not stop to plan, for they were too focused on what was about to happen. No one spoke; they just wondered aimlessly toward what was to be their demise or so Morkann plan was arranged.

They wandered through every trail, disappearing as thoroughly as water dried under the blazing, scorching heat of Sol Aureus and shades of solar flares. But James was watchful and felt his soul begin to freeze solid. Petrified with fear, he felt a sudden urge to wander forward past the strewn broken stars shimmering on the planet bed.

They just didn't have much time to stop and think about any of the other beings that they had met previously. How would they cope without the powerful and mammoth

Hakeem and his power and without Jambalee's guidance? There were too many questions, all of which whizzed around like a ball heading for a net. These two characters were the powerful ones, who could help them without asking. Lindiarna peeped over to her sons; lovingly, even though they were big enough to look after themselves, she made sure they were safe while trudging through the vibrantly colored cloud mist wafting in their path.

The family trudged on through the barren land hoping they would not fall into a solar whirlpool. Then, suddenly out from a shooting bright light, a minute fleck appeared spiraling towards the family.

"Get back James!" Natalya yelled pulling him back. Tom stopped as Lindiarna held him from his shoulder. The fleck of red light became brighter and stronger until a character emerged from the light source.

"This is Iktomi!" said Natalya introducing the proud warrior creature. The rough-skinned creature camouflaged against the cracked and broken boulder strewn around the loose ground. He wore a, red earthen robe half covering his strong muscular body.

The creature had red skin in his human form and stood proud. His body was transparent and it was possible to see his veins with a deep river of wine-colored liquid, which looked as if blood was flowing through. Like a tributary of blood all connected through his green and purple protruding veins.

The strange character stood full of pride, in his robe, tall, robust with a sculptured physique. His hair was shiny, black and long to his shoulders with his red skin marked with black rings around his dark eyes. His arms were strong and supple, built like a Italian sculpture.

"Who is he?" Asked the brothers said in unison. They were staring deeply at the powerful creature, which stood confident glaring back at the family.

The creature seemed from an ancient land. He was the trickster spirit, 'Iktomi'. "YOU Iktomi!" Lindiarna bellowed recognizing him straight away.

Natalya continued to glide away on ahead, witnessing the arrival of the trickster Iktomi.

"Have you changed for the better now? Or are you still wrapped in Morkann's wrath?" Lindiarna questioned.

"Who is he?" questioned Tom wearily asking his Mother.

Natalya, peering over to Iktomi, glared at him, gingerly.

"Iktomi is a shape shifter. He can use strings to control Carbonites like puppets. He will control you, if you let him". Natalya warned.

"Iktomi is the son of the Rock, a creator of spirits. However, Iktomi has a destructive and powerful spirit, and we must be watchful." Natalya said.

"Iktomi is the son of the Rock. He was known as 'Wisdom'. But he became foolish and did not yield his wisdom bestowed upon him by the creator of spirits. Instead he was frolicsome with his high order granted he was unable to sustain his power given and so the Spirits stripped him of his Wisdom and he became angry and then Iktomi the trickster was born, he was banished. It is very sad.

Because he held the company of the bad demons and foolish behavior he was consumed by the demon Morkann and became her slave."

"Wow that is sad. Can he ever go back?" queried James.

"No it is too late, but, I must tell you Iktomi had a younger brother, he was destructive with a powerful spirit. All the creatures and beings from the planets could not control him. I mean he was deadly but so Iktomi was let lose into the wilderness of stars." Natalya lectured

"But Iktomi's, appearance is that of a spider." James said cautiously.

"A spider! That's not very scary!" yelled Tom.

"Ah. But he can change very very quickly. Be wise, dear Princes." Said Natalya watching the trickster hover around the family. The lean, dark face had a hungry look to him, and his black hair fell down across his dark sunken eyes, which were circled with black markings.

"What will he do? Is going to hurt us?" asked Tom whilst watching him move around the ground.

"I don't know yet, we will have to see. I must warn you now, he has the ability to take any shape, including that of a mortal. He is a shape shifter. He has lost all wisdom to join the web of Morkann."

The creatures from the planets are frightened of Iktomi who is strong as a blade with his muscular torso and strong protruding physique on his arms and legs. When he would take his mortal state he will adorn the shades of war red, yellow and white paint, with black rings around his eyes. These are the powers of eternal life. Morkann, wanted to retrieve this for herself, so she took him as her slave servant, trying to steal his powers." Natalya warned.

"Yuck!" snapped Tom. The creature menacingly prowled around the family, snarling and snipping, as if to quickly take a bite with his wide, pale pink mouth. His eyes were deep and hollow, with black rings marked around his eyes. "You must watch out for his human form, the colors of Red, White and his black rings around his eyes." Natalya warned.

They were long and scrawny, yet the creature appeared strong, with his wide-open, terror-drenched, hollow eyes. Unexpectedly, it glared deeply into James's eyes before it intimidatingly mutated into a deadly serpent. Slowly slithering toward him, it lunged at the boys, roaring out furious flames of orange, blue, and yellow incandescent fire. It then opened its menacing jaw, bellowing the roar of a thousand lions, throwing the brothers away from getting any closer. Suddenly it thrust itself toward James, trying to catch a bite. The creature threw its fuming saliva-drenched mandible toward James and caught him clutching on to his leg, which looked like a sheer morsel for the beast. James froze, trying to yell out; he lost any volume he'd had in his voice. The creature seized James in its jaw, snapping it quickly shut, like a Venus fly trap. His huge eyes, now wild angry and red, examined the scene to see who would dare interrupt the monsters' wrath. James was tiring; his hands were confined, caught holding the sword that Tom had given him just moments before the monster had grabbed him. He pulled on the sword in the gilded hilt, struggling he, finally yanked the sword free. Tom, standing precariously between the mud-soaked rocks and boulders, watched in torment as the creature dangled James from its wretched jaw. Tom, not able to control his horror, clenched his fists until his fingernails dug painfully into his palms and he let out a loud scream, hoping he would be able to goad the monster toward him. Lindiarna stared at every move and action he was making and realised very quickly that the creature who transmuted into an abhorrent monster was Iktomi. He was the trickster from the old world and he was able to morph into anything he wanted to become. The creature was of the dark world, another world, yet sometimes he would change like a constellation melting into the galaxy and cross over into the good world of Oblivionarna. The creature was one of two molds, good and bad. Lindiarna hurriedly opened the magic pot, trying to throw grains of the white powder onto the deadly creature, her hands quivering and she trembled in trepidation. Tom continued to yell, trying desperately to scare the monster away, but to no avail. James, trying to lash out at the monster, raged as he tried in vain to strike with his sword. He swung his sword frantically, swinging it high toward the serpent's long scaly neck, several times. Like a fearless solider, his heart raced and thundered like a stereo unit turned on full blast. James's fight had now begun. Then the vicious creature raised his long scaly protruding neck high up into the galactic airspace, proudly displaying James in his mouth like a mere crumb. James threw his tired arm holding the sword toward the monster.

"Argh, I can't hold on... Tom DO something!" he yelled.

Tom roared out, "Mom! "We have to do something, I can't watch this—I have to do something!" Tom bellowed, "Someone do something, please! You have got to help James! James!" He turned to Natalya and yelled to her to do something as loud as he could, but to no avail.

Tom could only hear his brother screaming in agony. The empty moans and the anguish fell on to the ground with a discordant sound. James roared as he caught his sword on the serpent's limb. Deep purple liquid began to ooze slowly from the serpent's wound. James had swiped his sword and injured the creature, but it happened so quickly. The abhorrent creature was now injured and he knew it. It moaned in tumultuous dull groans. He glared at Tom, who was gawking with his waterlogged sore, red, raccoon eyes at every move the serpent made. The creature was angry and in pain. Still holding the sword, James struck the serpent again with all his might. This time he cut him with the sword, and the serpent reeled in deep pain. Lindiarna glanced at James quickly and leapt forward, her eyes now wide open in bewilderment and full of intense anxiety. She levitated, high up into the air toward the clouds, not knowing if she would come back alive. A white mist swallowed up her path as she glided to rescue her beloved son from the clutches of the monster's hungry jaw.

When Iktomi witnessed Lindiarna zoom up around him he didn't want James anymore, so the monster prepared to release him from his grip, swaying with James dangling from his salivating jaw. James glanced down at his hands and saw his knuckles, sore and red trying to escape from his hands. His palms became sticky and damp. He was unable to hold on to the sword from the angle he found himself in, and the gilded hilt fell onto the molten lava, shimmering its rays and forming a constellation high into the Milky-Way.

Although James was caught in Iktomi's jaw, Lindiarna plummeted towards the creature trying to snatch him back. Her face solemn and distraught, she could see her son and beast together. She flew at great speed toward them, skyrocketing into the air and locking her eyes with the monster. The monster Iktomi menacingly glared straight back, locking his hollow sultry black eyes into Lindiarna's sharp, sizzling green eyes. He gripped James tighter in his salivating jaw. As James had injured the serpent, Iktomi realised he no longer wanted James. There was a bigger feast to be had. He turned his gaze toward Lindiarna. The monster scowled at her intently. At that moment, Lindiarna quivered and blew into the skyline to move a constellation in anticipation of catching James from his fall. James, who had plopped from the monster's mouth, dropped like a fleck straight into the soft, invisible frame formed by a constellation of stars, emotionless. In desperation,

"You will need, your Latin Tom, he has been taken over by Morkann!" bellowed Natalya Tom wide-eyed stared at Iktomi and began to recite some of his Latin.

"Iktomi, Morkann Magister non vult malum!" "Iktomi, Morkann your Master does not wish you to harm him!

Lindiarna again threw some white magic powder in desperation toward Iktomi, and this time a few drops fell onto him.

"What did you say to him?" Lindiarna asked Tom puzzled.

"I just pretended my allegiance was with Morkann". Tom said. "And your master Morkann, does not wish you to hurt the mortal one!"

Suddenly, Iktomi the trickster transformed back into the little carbonite image being he once was again appearing in his red robe and long black shoulder length hair and muscular frame. Iktomi's arm was bleeding from where he had been cut with the sword when James had lashed out at him. Realising that he had been tricked, Iktomi became enraged. His ferocity became callous as Iktomi stared into Lindiarna's eyes with a deep frown The two creatures were once friends, yet as Iktomi did not yield his title as Wisdom, and became frivolous displaying much folly with the true facts his wisdom was stripped away. This caused much strife and he was taken away by Morkann and thus swallowed up by the demon world.

No words were spoken, but intrigue and jealousy flourished between Iktomi and Morkann.

Lindiarna was desperate, she tried again in vain to flick some of the grains onto Iktomi, but they only transformed into tiny frozen particles resembling minute sleet. This would then transform into magical atoms floating into the Milky-Way and subsequently into a cold, impervious sky. Lindiarna's face was an emotionless visage as she began to suddenly turn a pale shade of blue. Her lips were now trembling and her body quivering like fresh jelly straight from the fridge. She seeped into deep thoughtfulness of her life before she had landed on Earth and of her life now living on the planet. She feared that she would transform back to how she once appeared, as Lindiarna. The one who had the power of a supreme celestial faith could see she was now in the shadows of her demise.

Abruptly, a dark gray shadowy mist smothered the surround, and as the family glared into the sky, the thick gray smog fell over their sight. Their eyes were now wide open, anticipating that all was not well. In horror they all precipitously were swept high up into a whirlwind tornado, catching everything within its wrath.

Temperatia was back as herself. The gray smoldering smog molded into wild shapes of the darkness and evil as malicious Morkann was resurrected. Her strands of Medusa hair swayed like snakes sliding on each comet, snatching at the stars. The colors around her were in angry shades of red and orange, with iridescent blues dazzling like hidden diamonds. No longer was she Morkann but only the wild wind trying to cause havoc and suffocate the family. In doing so, she swept up James into her path.

"Argh... let go!" He yelled out into space, but no one could hear him. He looked down through the revolving wind to see fragments of Iktomi hobbling away holding his arm; he appeared to be twisting in agony. James knew he had managed to slice his neck with his sword. Now, Iktomi was back to himself, the long scaly neck must of been his arm. He wasn't proud, but everything was fair in war. Iktomi was holding his lacerated arm, when thick brown liquid began to gently ooze onto his small torso.

"What have you done?" he snarled, glaring up with menacing eyes. James became cautious, yet he always felt Iktomi was a trickster. He turned to see his master, Morkann. It was Morkann who was the controlling the trickster, like a puppet, along with her many ghouls. Morkann or the wrath of Temperatia was intent in throwing her power to cause mayhem and destruction. Iktomi levitated over James, knowing of his distrust Iktomi spoke sarcastically, "Listen carefully; listen to me, dear mortal. The mortal world will see many disasters, typhoons, tornadoes, and volcano eruptions on a scale that it will not be to sustain. Morkann, my queen will cause floods and many mortal-world catastrophes. Her torrent of waves of hideous destruction will return to our planet to cause natural explosions and meteoroids to shoot out in our land, while space would be a determent to the mortal world, causing destruction on a colossal scale." Iktomi whined.

James listened while the haunting chants of dead and broken stars rolled in with the silent mist, a thousand voices whispering a cacophony all at once, demanding attention but not being understood.

"This is all to scare you both and you're Mother." Iktomi sniggered sarcastically and then proclaimed Morkann as his true queen. James frowned and took a short glance down at his Mother in defiance, hoping she would be able to scare them away or say anything or do anything with her many powers.

"You must remember, James; life and death are in the power of the tongue. Who knows the way out of a maze you cannot see the beginning of?" warning James, Lindiarna peered into her sons' eyes. "The enemy is closer than your soul.

86

Chapter IV
Iktomi Returns

(This chapter contains Latin)

I ktomi scuffed towards James and Lindiarna and in doing so Tom caught Iktomi's glance which instantly resulted in Iktomi the devious trickster revealing his intentions. He quickly shot his open eyes towards Lindiarna retuning his gaze with a deep stare. Now Iktomi's face no longer resembled that of a dragon as he had slowly transmuted back, watching the strange creature transform was to see the color first melt into a pale shade of sodium as if to blend into the ground they all stood upon like a chameleon, then transmuted into the little frail being they had first met. Tom saw it the trickster had revealed himself as he once was.

"You don't seem happy -Lindiarna?" Iktomi suggested with a sardonic smile as he squinted his dark eyes. Lindiarna stood like a proud statuesque figure in the distant unforgiving wasteland. The harsh sand colored dusty wind brushed against her body wiping her face with

87

its sodium colored haze. This was the stark land which she had once left behind. The planet was an ancient galaxy that had collided with futuristic horizons and where rocky sharp spires then sliced the abyss shooting short florescent illuminating flickers of light to float and vanish in to the galactic airspace. This was otherwise known as 'Shooting – stars'. Lindiarna silently gazed through the floating vibrant colored stars on to the forbidden barren land before her. Tom still watching Iktomi's intentions nudged James at his discovery, bewildered they both starred at the strange devious character. Iktomi, scowling at both boys and with his sly slithery whining voice spoke,

"This was where it was once suggested; when the land was young, a humongous explosion collided with the future purple horizon and after much upheaval many lands separated causing the beings of that land and beast to be dispersed across the various orbits.

This of course created a gauge of dunes and mountainous ridges all forming openings with rocky canyons. They created large and small ravines with pernicious sand dunes whilst precious turquoise, shimmering liquid formed rivulets through its hazardous terrain dispersing the jewels of turquoise stones and emerald gems shimmer in the ravine".

James was totally aghast at the wilderness before him. He no longer thought of his love, Princess Anna-Lisa. James was completely mesmerized by Iktomi's transformation. All he could do now was to watch Iktomi parade in this brutal place wondering if he could be trusted or not and if they would survive with the great trickster looking after them and at their side.

Iktomi turned to face the family and hobbled closer toward them. He no longer seemed to be frightened of them, and he tried not to scare the family too. He turned to face Lindiarna and proudly spoke,

"You maybe in your land Lindiarna but much has changed, there are now hostile mounds and spirits which lurk in the liquid languishing in the crevices of the boulders fallen from Moradiya. Temperatia-Morkann is slowly reinstating more power — you realise that, Don't you; blood for blood Lindiarna?" Pausing with a forlorn gaze through his hollow red eyes he slowly questioned Lindiarna who had become startled and shocked.

Lindiarna and James turned to each other. It was obvious that James did not trust Iktomi, how could he? After, all he was a trickster; Iktomi had tried to kill him on their first encounter. James appeared puzzled and very nervous, yet curious about even entertaining such a strange, character or would be friend. James head jerked up." I have to put straight to you, I don't trust you!". Iktomi, frowned looking at his hands, there were hurt, and the awkward way he held them, the raw red scars and dry blood from the last two fingers.

"So, Iktomi, tell me, I am intrigued, why don't I believe you are going to help us?" James questioned incredulously.

Tom watched his older brother glare at Iktomi intently but remained silent. Iktomi, noticed Tom constant gaze," You are the younger one and are wise to remain silent, yet you have a question. . He asked in a slippery voice.

Lindiarna glanced over at James. She knew that it would be incredible if James was going to trust him. She paused and gradually dipped her eyes as if to summon someone higher to help. In that moment, a purple meteor zipped through the orbit at great speed. Everyone looked up into the chasm depth of the airspace. All around them everything was floating or zooming with different color Nebula's were in view. The fire red Nebula was perhaps the most spectacular of all. Iktomi quickly realising this was his chance to try and convince the family of his loyalty, through is limp arm, which seemed to have grown miraculously about two meters longer around them. He gathered together the perplexed family and then moved them quickly towards a broken boulder strewn on the planet.

James still in disbelief broke free from the character. 'What are you doing?' Tom straightened up and Lindiarna suddenly began to feel tightness in her arms. Although she was half listening to the discussion between her boys and Iktomi she broke away from the group and walked a few steps back from the where they were standing. Lindiarna realised that the world she had left behind had changed. It seemed the Lupans were no longer free and there was no sign of Jambalee, Halaconia or even Hakeem.

Lindiarna lost in ponder, gazed around the iridescent orbit she now stood in front of. All that she was able to see was large floating remnants of a meteorite that was reaching the surface of a planet because it was not disintegrating completely in the atmosphere. She witnessed the bright light left to decay in fluorescent colors and strange shapes, red, lime, orange and a deep purple all dangling twinkling and shinning in varied angular shapes.

Her loyal servant Jambalee appeared and with him at his side the Unicorn James had saved from his certain death and the fearless Halaconia, standing proud with her silver wings stretched wide. Both Jambalee and Halaconia smiled as if they had reached their destination. Tom from the corner of his eye could see his Mom's relief as the distant familiar sight of faces grew nearer towards them. Lindiarna's eyes lit up and as they did rivulets of tears dripped from her confused face. She gave a welcome smile whilst breathing a sigh of relief. A conundrum of thoughts splashed through her mind darting fragments of her childhood as she reminisced her past.

Not knowing to smile or to smile she gazed directly at the strange beings approaching her.

Although it had been many years since Lindiarna had seen Jambalee, she knew instantaneously that it was her loyal servant.

As Jambalee, Halaconia and the Unicorn approached it was what Lindiarna had expected. There the little

'Lupan' stood. He was brave, fearless in his strange brown coat, which clearly looked as if it were too big for him, yet it appeared ageless. The darkness of the surround dotted between flickering stars created a kaleidoscope of brightcolors bouncing off from Lindiarna's face and then towards both James and Tom's face.

Seeing the Unicorn, James excitedly sprinted to his side, patting and stroking it quite hard and nuzzling it closely trying to convince him of why he was delayed on his return, 'There... there... it's okay... you're okay now...I'm back' James lovingly patted the Unicorn, whilst caressing and stroking the neck of the slender muscular Unicorn, trying to control and reassure him. The beast nuzzled up closely, creating a vibrating sound with his mouth, his eyes beamed up at James. It was obvious that the Unicorn had missed his master. James identifying that he was being greeted, stroked and patted his fur coat. He watched intently as the Unicorn dipped his large topaz almond shaped eyes releasing a single tear, nuzzling closely into James's shoulder. James, wondered where Princess Anna-Lisa was. Both Lindiarna and Tom watched intently knowing that the bond between both James and the Unicorn was still very strong almost unique and appeared quite remarkable.

"Come ... show me where the Princess is..." James pulled the Unicorn's neck towards him glaring at his silver horn. The Unicorn did not have the power of voice, so he bowed and allowed his horn to shimmer as Tom too began to stroke the Unicorn. James was able to sense a lost thought and turned to Halaconia for reassurance. The bright Dillyan, she was betrothed to the handsome Aspero, the fearless Dillyan army leader. Halaconia was beautiful, with her dusky complexion and her long curly aubergine hair pulled to one side of her face covering the flowers of a ginger Lilly emerging on the right-side of her appearance. She was delicate and her feet were hooves, poised locked like ballerina's dainty feet.

"Tell me please, Halaconia, what has happened to Princess Anna-Lisa, where is she now? James asked worriedly, as Iktomi cut into the conversation. "James, James, your Princess is imprisoned in the Tower of Doom, Belle á Noir once more. The first thing my queen Morkann, did was to separate the Unicorn from her side. And you know the Unicorn has many special powers, so she could not just kill him". Iktomi stared at James as he turned sharply to face him, "How do you know?"

Halaconia, interrupted frowning at Iktomi, "James, she is alive I am sure and I am sure she awaits your return".

"She was taken shortly after you returned to your Earth; the Gods know how she tried not to be taken prisoner. After the death of Morkann's father, the wicked King Polydectes, she took vengeance on all.

James, frowned with a deep sorrow, feeling helpless and more determined to find her alive.

Tom deliberated, cautiously peering around the purple starlit horizon. He gazed up at his older brother's playful interaction with his beloved Unicorn. He felt it safe that he was also able to stroke the powerful white slender smooth coat of the rescued majestic creature. As Tom stepped forward to stroke the creature's slender neck he began to wonder notice the Unicorn's silver horn sparkling in the twilight sky something was not quite right he thought. Although the surround was strange something was about to happen and Tom could sense it the Unicorn's horn confirmed it by shimmering brightly in a carousel of colors. He closed his eyes tightly for a spilt second turnaround swiftly to glance at his Mother and then he walked towards the white muscular Unicorn. Tom's eyes shifted nervously as the Unicorn shuffled and neighed loudly before Tom could grab his neck to guide him into position. Tom, James and Jambalee quickly glimpsed up at the peculiar heavy shadow now enveloping the airspace, around them. They all squinted and frowned in astonishment, wondering what was happening. Lindiarna scaled the horizon, but she had not lived on the planet for a very long time and so the strange happenings were just stranger!

It seemed to be hovering over the luminous gaseous stars. Iktomi froze, licking his lips, clearly contemplating his next action. It appeared Iktomi was not as anxious as the others. Whilst Jambalee knew something was clearly wrong, he tried to usher both boys and Lindiarna towards a large fracture in the planet acting like a cave. Jambalee watched cautiously as they all stepped towards the crevice.

He peered back at the Unicorn, 'Look! Why is he blowing like that!' Tom asked anxiously.

'What does that mean then?' questioned Tom again inquisitively.

'When the Unicorn blows like that at something he usually is curious, I think he is also aware of the Galzar!'

Lindiarna began to speak to Halaconia in Latin, "*Quod fuerit longum tempus, Ut diu Halaconia fidelis es, qui fuit. Veni abscondam hic nobiscum.*" She said in Latin it has been a long time, Halaconia - you are loyal as ever. Come, you will hide here with us". Lindiarna greeted her with a big smile and held her hands tightly.

Halaconia lowered her lashes in respect to the truthful Queen, Lindiarna as she spoke. Although Halaconia was in awe of Lindiarna she listened intently. Halaconia began to flap her silver transparent wings, trying to take flight. Yet for some reason she could not. Something now was making it very difficult for her to take flight. She frowned nervously and looked up at Lindiarna as if she were asking for her help.

They were all now hiding in the dark moss covered crevice strewn with thick strands of green lichen. The vines dripped like fallen tears beckoning each person who wanted to live to embrace it as a form of survival.

'Zonal, barked James, that's the ammonia clouds from Jupiter – over there?' James pointed excitedly.

Tom then quickly retorted, "Your right, James that's it! That's the one and that's with its powerful storms!" Both brothers turned to each other and in unison, "Temperatia!" James grinned at Tom, it was that eureka moment they had concluded. James continued his diagnosis of the cloud now covering the tor. That's the cloud storm, Jambalee, it's her Morkann. They are always accompanied by those blue white lightning strikes. The storms are a result of her evil, moist convection in the atmosphere connected to the evaporation and condensation of water. They are the sites of a strong upward motion from the carbonite air, which leads to the formation of bright and dense clouds. These storms form mainly in the belt regions, they will protect her army before she strikes. The crimson and blue bolts of lightning strikes and sudden golden light flashes you see on the planet Jupiter are more powerful than those you have on your Earth. "You are what we call, Carbonites, Mortals from a planet that does not see right from wrong".

"Hold on, I wouldn't say we are all like that!" James protested.

"Yes you are right my formidable prince, however, there are fewer of you, which hold your conviction."

"Temperatia, Morkann, the dark demon queen is as you are aware, a phenomenal creature, she has held her wrath since the the death of King Polydectes, her father. Jambalee continued with a heavy sigh peering up at a nervous Tom who was listening intently.

Lindiarna glanced over at Jambalee's comments; she glared at the abyss chasm in front of her. Yet there was no light to be seen only the frozen white clouds in the form of strange shape asteroids floating in an obscure manner, Lindiarna and her boys were now locked in their shadow in a corner of hidden cove between the planet's cave.

There is no life here that meets the eye!' Jambalee retorted, protectively huddling Halaconia and the Unicorn deeper into the cave.

"Never allow what you are looking at to determine what you believe, my dear Carbonites!" 'Never allow what you can see with your eyes to lure you into the belief that there is nothing more. Alas, allow your spiritual eyes to take you beneath the surface"

Jambalee finished rhyming whilst glaring deeply at Lindiarna. Both James and Tom with Halaconia felt a presence of a cold stillness pour through the cave at that very moment. The sharp wind was biting and nipped at the ears of both brothers.

"Argh!" Tom yelled as he hurriedly threw his palms over his ears trying to stop the icy wind bite at them. His lips inflated and his eyes frowned, whilst his hands turned a bright red. James yelled out whilst trying to bow down to avoid the biting wave. He shook and dropped his shoulders, also trying to protect his ears. Grimacing James tried to stop the Unicorn from jumping up and began to calm him down whilst watching James in pain. Halaconia could but watch as her wings were frozen. Upset and agitated, whilst

97

wiping her wings as if to bring them to life she peered at Jambalee in despair.

"So what next? What's happening?" squealed an angry Halaconia, who seemed annoyed at her wings refusal to come alive. Jambalee thoughtfully walked over to the void within the clearing of the cove. He glared over at the wispy white Unicorn and the strong teenagers together with Lindiarna, 'We must enter the terrain before us most prudently, for if not we will come across the chilling dark galaxies of Galzar; Lindiarna listening intently gazed deeply into Jambalee's eyes, "So what if we try to escape?" she questioned anxiously. Jambalee gave a half smile and replied assertively,

"Then we will undoubtedly fall into the galaxy of Rexorum (of the Kings) and with its entire fury that will accompany it."

Everyone looked stunned at Jambalee's comments, "So what are we going just sit here, and wait for the destruction?" queried James angrily.

"The Galzarian portal is something we must be conscious of, for it will be our greatest battle yet!" Jambalee insisted.

"But for now we are trapped on the fringes of Tumblewood". Jambalee paused glancing around at the Milk-Way iridescent horizon. Tom peered at him closely. He was after all a strange looking creature, with his purple spiky hair and his too tight buttoned coat or jacket; He really was a puzzle. James still stroking his beloved Unicorn stopped whilst watching Halaconia fiddle with her wings, she was so beautiful albeit her being small. James always had a soft spot for her, so he walked over softly asking, "Do want some help?"

James asked as he watched her gently trying to straighten her silver wings as they drooped and fell onto the sodium colored dust covering ground. She peered up to James, with her bright wide open gazelle shaped Amber eyes, fluttering her eyes lashes like a cartoon character,

"Not sure what you will be able to do, but go on". She replied anixiously releasing her hold on her wings James held the silver wing. It felt heavy and tired he began to gently massage the wing. Halaconia began to scrutinize James's action and smiled nervously, she knew James was once smitten with her despite her wings and hooved feet. He released it back to her, "Take this", James said handing over her massaged wing.

"James, I can feel my wing..." There was a pause and before she could continue the Unicorn lifted and jolted jumping up on his hind legs neighing loudly. Lindiarna and Jambalee gazed cautiously through the cove further from where they were all hiding inside. There was a dull rush and gush sound of liquid as they both peered they could see an inky sapphire blue ocean surge and swell and it was heading towards the cove where they were all in hiding.

'Quick! We all have to get out of here now!' Jambalee bellowed. They both took a deep breath, looking at each other; their eyes open wide like nocturnal animals. There was a short silence enough to contemplate who was now raging their wrath. James grabbed Halaconia by her petit hand and told her to sit on the Unicorn, whilst Jambalee navigated a way out of the cove without being hit by Temperatia's ocean storm heading their way.

The Unicorn again jolted and then unexpectedly blew and as he did so his horn started to glisten and shimmer in a dazzling silver white light. It became effervescent and appeared holy, both James and Tom were aghast, watching in glee.

All that was now visible beneath its surface was a dark eerie shadow languishing in obscure shapes, and then there it was the towering rage of blue white tide slashing the jagged rock of the cove.

"Look—out!" Tom howled to anyone who was near him. There was a sudden madness everyone was running in the small space as the Unicorn jumped out of the cove and into the air, his horn twinkled a luminous orange. Halaconia was still sat on the Unicorn's back holding on to its silver thick mane with all her might, trying aimlessly to free her wings from the discomfort.

"Argh. my wings!" she screamed. Tom grabbed the Unicorn by his long white silver tail quickly clambering on as they moved slowly through the strange surreal galactic landscape. Tom could see clearly a blue green sky punctured by broken stars shimmering in the dark void of deep space.

James, Lindiarna with Jambalee were caught up in the stillness of the magical surround. A gush of sapphire green, ocean froze over into a cotton wool sky as constellations danced and bounced off the edge of Tumblewood, it was an Aurora Borealis of space.

The whole episode took only but a few moments, however, it felt like hours had past. Lindiarna turned to Jambalee for reassurance,

"Are we in Oblivionarna, Tumblewood?" she questioned restlessly.

"We are, much as changed Lindiarna, so much has changed!" Jambalee replied with a gloomy visage, and then he let out a sigh of sorrow.

"What is it Jambalee? What has happened?" Questioned a puzzled and ever inquisitive Lindiarna She frowned in deep sorrow.

"You must not use your cosmic patterns to change the flow of life Lindiarna. The planets have changed and Morkann has set her goals for destruction". Natalya said with a skeptical look.

"When the poison for King Cepheus was administered, many Lupans, Dillyans and Orags and creatures were astonished that the poison took so long to take hold. We all knew and the shaman tried to intervene but he was changed to stone!" Lindiarna gasped, placing her hand upon her lips in disbelief and horror.

"It was a slow death, one that should not have been visible — to any eye — be that of a Carbonite or creature." Jambalee said lamentably.

Chapter V
Temperatia Quest

Temperance allows nature full play, with temperance;
nature can exert herself in all her force and vigour.
—J Addison
(This Chapter contains Latin)

There were sporadic tufts of trees, acacia and thorn trees, wild and sharp, with loose vines sprawled across the boulders of broken comets that had fallen to the ground. It was like goodness had tried to show its path once more. Patchy grasses and shrubs topped the brown earthen crust, a surface that looked as hard as stone and somehow even less inviting. There was a hazy orange dust everywhere— on leaves, branches, and even on Lindiarna's teeth and lips. She kissed the dust away and started brushing it from her clothes. She gently glanced up at both her sons. James in particular was visibly disturbed from his ordeal with Iktomi when he metamorphosed into a serpent.

Lindiarna glanced around her immediate surroundings. There was a silent mist soaking up the orange horizon, making the air damp and moist. Lindiarna, amazed at how the planet appeared eerily dormant, and still rubbed away any last remnants of dust that had fallen covering her eyes. She gently wiped away the last few grains smudged upon her face. She was now able to see her sons clearly. She called to them to check if they were safe. They all stood still, watching the horizon drain of color in the squash-colored sky. Lindiarna knew instantly that they had arrived in Moradiya. This was the dismal planet of everything bleak and evil. If there was anything strange and evil, it was always going to be found on this land. The land of Morkann is - Moradiya.

"Oh, how this land has changed," Lindiarna pondered, muttering to herself. Lost in deep thought, she began to advise her sons that they should not verge to close to the Valley of Doom, which held the colossal tower Belle á Noir. This tower pierced the very skyline created and it had no windows only a tiny break along the black old mottled broken stars, now appearing like tatty bricks piled so high. This was the tower of death.

"You see that there?" she said, pointing to the humungous, overpowering, hideous black tower protruding out of the ground like an erupting mole tunnel.

Both James and Tom gasped, they could not help but notice the darkness that fell from the tower overshadowing the skyline. It appeared as though the Grim Reaper had set up home comfortably.

"This is the place where the Princess Anna-Lisa is being kept, I am sure of it, along with anyone else who Morkann wants out of her way."

"Well, is she still there?" James questioned eagerly.

"I don't know. We will see, you have the potion pot? Just watch out for the ghouls," Lindiarna answered.

They continued to trudge through the terrain, passing a weeping Lupan who seemed to have been injured.

"Help, help…help me," his little voice begged. Tom knelt down as Lindiarna and James watched him.

"What's happened?" Tom questioned, placing his hand onto his little, bedraggled shoulder.

The little creature had been injured in a fierce battle, and after he spoke, Tom shook his head.

"She has more wrath than evil itself! You must watch for the silver shimmer one, he…he…is the one…" The Lupan, who resided on the planet of Oblivionarna wept, and his voice faded until he was dead. Tom quickly looked up at James. They were shocked and scared that the battle had begun and that it was very real. Tom closed the Lupan's eyes and placed him carefully into the corner of the ditch so that he would not be disturbed. It was a sad moment and all were silent.

"You know, my sons, the best and beautiful things on this planet cannot be seen or even touched, but they must be felt in your heart. That goes for you particularly, James, when you meet Princess Anna–Lisa." Lindiarna gave a disconcerting look to James, trying to communicate the dangers ahead.

They all continued cautiously along the grey ground laden with black lava ash among the fallen blue and green stars withering away, flashing their lights for a slumber. Lindiarna grabbed onto a thick hanging lichen vine swaying from a gargantuan rock that was strewn nearby. The ground dappled with hard molten dry lava and protruding roots, between each branch there was a small sprig of a black flower, with its leaves hanging limp in the grey, damp air.

She could feel his pain and that his land of Moradiya now too was under threat.

Iktomi walked over to the brothers, swaying like an injured animal, taunting them. His arms were bare, long, and strong. He seemed to be in a euphoric mood. Iktomi was throwing his, arms around while dropping his legs like a spider. Lindiarna scowled with her lips tightly compressed. She gazed at Iktomi. Her sons were simply astounded at the weird creature. They all watched flabbergasted. She glared up at him and nervously spoke out, "Iktomi, it has been a long time. Why are you scaring us? We bring you no harm."

Both brothers gawked at their Mother, this of course was the first time they had seen their Mother in the land she had left behind. Lindiarna was concerned how her two sons, now young men, would be able to survive on the planet. They could see it in the creases on her forehead as she frowned and in the slight pressure in her lips, causing it to pout gently in anguish.

Like the purr of a puma lunging at its prey, Iktomi glared deeply at the family, gazing intently at Lindiarna and at her boys. Iktomi had mutated back into his spider self and stopped throwing his angular arms and hands around. He shook as if to throw the toxin of a black Widow spider gawping as he walked closer to the family. His eyes were round and bulging from his face. He was a spider, deadly and was able to change into anything at great speed. He stood in the shape of a Black Widow Spider, with his raccoon eyes bulging out of his obscure countenance. Iktomi jumped into a crevice, the minutes later jumped out as a human figure. His fingers were long and thin, so that each bone was possible to see through the stretchy dark red skin. "You!" He heckled loudly to Lindiarna. "Why are you back?" he questioned surreptitiously with malice in his voice. He was angry, but Lindiarna was unable to determine why he was so acrimonious in his outburst.

"Temperatia will not be happy, but you don't care!" he bawled sardonically in a raspy voice, stretching each word as he spoke.

"I bring you no harm. Why do you fear me so, Iktomi? You know I have been absent from this land for many years. I come only to take my rightful throne. King Cepheus was

107

your king. Do you forget that?" Lindiarna said calmly but in great trepidation.

There was a deathly silence as the creature maneuvered into an abstract position. Natalya, levitated toward Iktomi, "Iktomi, you were known as Wisdom, now where has it gone?" She asked trying to gage his attention. Lindiarna peered deeply into Iktomi's round, bulging eyes. His strong frame somehow didn't match up to the venomous monster that he had transformed into earlier. He levitated across the ubiquitous ground of scattered, luminous crystals that mingled with craters and fallen star debris from Jupiter and Mercury planets. James and Tom, together with Lindiarna, glared at their surroundings. Iktomi commented, "I know you do not wish to be here. I know it!" snapped Iktomi.

Lindiarna turned sharply to Iktomi.

"Iktomi, I have no choice. No longer can my life as a Carbonite be sustained".

"But you...," he continued, slyly hovering around Lindiarna. "We know that the planets represent the primary energies of life, but they are falling, and if they fall anymore, they could be swallowed up by the Crater of Death!"

"Iktomi! You were 'Wisdom". Why have you not learnt your lesson?" Lindiarna said trying to reason with the creature.

Natalya, watched discerningly at the tricksters next sly move.

"But why would I let that happen?" Lindiarna retaliated, startled at his assumption. "Iktomi, you must follow the path of right and truth. I know Sol Aureus's moon will die, I am aware of this!" she said defiantly. "And yes, this is why I have come back." Lindiarna paused as her emerald-green eyes lowered only for a second. She desperately wanted to help her planet, and in her last attempt, she turned, clenching onto the thought of Iktomi helping them against Morkann.

"Morkann will destroy us and the planets—you do know that?" she said pleading with the creature. Lindiarna looked horrified at the anguish of Iktomi.

"Iktomi, I wish I could help you, but you are with the ghouls the Morkannis now and Temperatia, Morkann. They control you now. Iktomi, it was King Cepheus gave you power! He treated you well—remember?"

Tom and James were aghast at the strange creature and his antics. James felt uneasy about him and being around him. They watched the obscure being as he listened attentively. Tom felt he would be able to do something and thus persuade Iktomi to their aid.

Their conversation slowly faded as Iktomi swayed closer. James blinked, trying to adjust his eyes to the purple nimble light source, dispersing its sharp shadows onto the falling crater. It gently illuminated the surroundings, and both young men suddenly ducked to protect themselves from the falling shards and debris from the meteor shower. Tom rose from the heavy boulder he was hiding behind, and James cautiously stood, still gazing high into the horizon.

"Who! What was that?" snapped James.

"Hmm, it is the rain of falling stars, the ones who were unable to grow into the new planet," Iktomi replied, humbled by the two young men now trying to save their planet.

Iktomi smiled, a devious smile levitating toward James.

"You, James, cannot help the creatures of Moradiya. The stars and planets are constantly falling, in the sense that they do not continue straight in their current direction! Like you humans, mortal carbonites, - they die. The planets fall tangential, or perpendicular to, the sun. They are constrained to curve around the great Sol Aureus moon, where they continue to be led into a curve rather than to travel in a straight line, as a carbonite body in motion." Iktomi gave a wry smile while seeming to be relieved that the two young men from Earth were now asking questions about his land. "I am pleased you seem keen to know of our land, your Mother has taught you well for a Carbonite!" Iktomi snarled as he hovered slyly around the family. James had taken an instant dislike to the strange obscure creature, which seemed to be always slithering around them.

James was not happy with the chameleon creature or his antics. Iktomi snarled back at him in the hope that he would go. There was something that kept James at a distance. He just didn't like him. James began to clench his jaws when he spoke to Iktomi.

"I didn't like you when we first met. But you have a habit of reappearing. I know you're a trickster but we just came to rescue the princess and help my Mom," James barked making his distrust evident.

Tom shook his head in disbelief at James's outburst, and Lindiarna interrupted quickly. "Iktomi, we mean you no harm; please let us be on our way.

Lindiarna was skeptical as she elevated, floating between the purple mists past the falling, illuminated constellations.

"Why did you try to kill us earlier?" Tom asked.

"You are an inquisitive Carbonite" Iktomi said.

Iktomi turned his back and slowly walked away. He was still injured, although his wound had congealed. In an urgent murmur, Iktomi muttered, "Were you scared? He asked hoping for the answer he wanted to hear. I like it when you are scared?"

James grimaced, finding Iktomi's comment quite disconcerting. It was clear that James did not trust Iktomi in the way perhaps he should have done; after all, he was a trickster with many faces.

James quickly turned to Tom, whispering, "Is this for real? Do you trust him?"

At that moment, Iktomi hearing the conversation turned to face them.

Snarling he moaned, "Why do you not trust me? My world is to be destroyed, and Temperatia does not care. I will do anything, anything for you, sire!" His voice trailed off and became softer as he tried to persuade the family to trust him. Iktomi squirmed as he slithered toward James.

James was unsure of the creature and indeed his intentions with his lip turned up, he glared at the strange creature one more time. There was something that nagged at the very edge of his consciousness. Tom was not deterred by Iktomi, and he turned to his Mother, Lindiarna, for reassurance. He peered intently to Iktomi replying,

"Iktomi, you tried to kill my brother. What do you now expect us to do?" He lowered his eyebrows and squeezed his eyes to try and gain some answers from this weird creature. "You can't answer, can you?" Tom bawled.

James watched from the corners of his eyes as Tom questioned waiting for a reply from the malignant creature.

Iktomi hobbled around the ground like a schoolteacher seeking his pupil. He answered, "You do not know this is a brutal place, and you may not last long."

Lindiarna shot her eyes directly at the strange creature, and both James and Tom were now under the impression Iktomi was going to help them.

"I promise I won't use my neurotoxins on you." Smirking Iktomi snapped back at the family.

The family smiled and lackadaisically listened to Iktomi. "I am going to help you, yes. You may not like my methods, but I'll help you," he said in a raspy voice.

At that moment, in a sudden puff of gray smoke, Iktomi transmuted into a fierce, mighty, imperviously scaled creature that was able to blow vibrant flames of fire —a large, obnoxious, scaly dragon now stood before a horrified James and Tom. They watched intently. Their eyes were wide open like a midnight owl's, fixated on the creature's transformation. He swished his long, heavy scaly tail like a cedar displaying his bones, protruding like beams of bronze. The sinews of his thighs were tightly knit, and his ribs appeared like iron. Iktomi had become a danger to all around him, perhaps even to himself. The deep-grey encrusted dragon, with its webbed, triangular black feet and slimy, thorny green scales tried to treacherously goad the family toward him. Iktomi didn't look menacing, but he did appear very powerful. His eyes were large, round, and bright, topaz in color, and sparkling as a gateway to a magnificent mystical chamber. Neither, James, Tom or Lindiarna was unable to look away, as they were fixated on the creature's wrath. Was he a friend or foe? James was puzzled and confused as to whether this creature was something they could rely on as a friend or not.

Then the dragon let out a tumultuous roar in a clear, powerful voice. "You must jump onto my shoulders, and I will take you around the planet of Moradiya to see what is needed of you," Iktomi bellowed.

Lindiarna swallowed up her intense gaze, nodding to her sons cautiously, acknowledging his command for them to jump onto the strange creature's back. James still waited through another lengthy silence, his mind flooding with questions, yet he heaved himself quietly onto to the innocuous creature.

The brothers soon settled on the shoulders of the strange dragon, and Iktomi leapt into the Milky-way. It was an abyss, a labyrinth of darkness except for a beam of fluorescent yellow fire light streaming through the galactic airspace. They were now flying, higher than space itself, gliding into a vortex cloud through an abyss. All that could be seen was strange floating craters and planets of obscure time. James waited for Iktomi to speak.

"Look, humans," Iktomi said, his voice sounding as if he were speaking through an amplifier. His voice began to reverberate into space before trailing off into nowhere. James snarled at Iktomi, shooting up his gaze into the creature's body.

"No one remains at a constant distance in a circular orbit, but they will fall and gain speed, which affords them the energy to climb to a higher position. This is aphelion versus perihelion, but not a higher orbit nor lower." Iktomi, although now metamorphosed into a sultry dragon, spoke with a deep and powerful slippery voice that reverberated, through the tor.

"Tut..., do you believe him? I don't trust him, that's for sure." James was adamant; he felt Iktomi was not a righteous character and a real trickster.

Tom listened intently, and Lindiarna jumped in cautiously to finish Iktomi's explanation.

"Iktomi, if you are going to help us, then you have to let me finish, before it is too. Their behavior is often explained as gravity and the conversion between potential energy. That's the height and kinetic energy—movement," Lindiarna said. "I knew this would happen; Morkann, or Temperatia, has been intent on ruling the planets. Iktomi replied. "Everything she has ever done has always been to scare me away!" Lindiarna retorted as she became dismayed.

"Lindiarna, King Polylectedes is no more, and so the Temperatia, or Morkann, as you know her to be, only has you and the Lupans in her way of ruling the galaxies. This reflects—how you say—the *'Newtonian'*, properties of the planet and action at a distance," Iktomi bellowed.

The creature continued speaking in a loud, piercing gruff. Iktomi was indeed a trickster, only Lindiarna had to decide whether he could be trusted or not. Lindiarna was half listening, until Natalya finally snapped at Iktomi's explanation. "If you are going to view the Orbit as space-time around the Sol Aureus, it will be distorted by its mass, allowing the planet to be seen as following the natural path of at least resistance and least energy! You know that, right?"

Tom then interrupted worriedly realising his Mother was not happy with the untrustworthy trickster Iktomi. He continued, "Which is deflected around the Sol Aureus, forming a bowl or well. Perfect, I think we understand this completely, Iktomi!"

James frowned with deep anxiety. He was not amused; thinking how this trickster first tried to kill him and now he seemed to have befriended his brother as well as his Mother.

"Iktomi, I don't understand any of this jargon, but I want to ask you, how can we trust you?"

It seemed that no matter what or how Iktomi spoke, nothing would sit right with him as far as Iktomi was concerned. He was a trickster.

Lindiarna frowned, and although they were all now perched and gliding on the back of the scaly dragon, they suddenly saw the cut in Iktomis' limb that James had made using his sword, when Iktomi was struck.

Iktomi too, although a powerful trickster in his own right, was in pain.

"Look!" Iktomi bellowed as he surged past the red planet with a display of fierce contention. It was heavily dense with small potholes. Out sprang shoots of short, orange short sodium flames, illuminating the chasm leading to the planet Oblivionarna. "This is your land, Lindiarna!" The dragon pointed with his vibrant, bat-like wing to the oval-shaped land, illuminating its sporadic silver ultraviolet sapphire lights.

They all headed for the cryptic land of Oblivionarna, the land Lindiarna had left behind and where Lupans reigned in peace. She gazed intently. Something nagged at the edge of her consciousness. Tom scrutinizing his Mother very carefully something did not sit right with Tom, and his subconscious processes forced him to shut down, let his mind go blank, and work on the problem he now faced. He turned away and quickly glared back at James. They all gently descended precariously, from the scaly, furious, dragon, the trickster beamed back as Iktomi. He glared straight at James from the corner of his diamond-shaped topaz eyes as his black markings shimmered around the sockets of his eyes. As they all disembarked from the dragon, Iktomi transformed back into the weird being that he was. No words were spoken to the creature why would any word uttered resonate with this strange being?

Iktomi sneered at Lindiarna and her sons as they wandered into the terrain. They then all trudged on silently through the sloshy, mulch-ridden ash -ridden landscape. It had become dense and was littered with silver fallen stars fighting through to light its intensity. They were glistening and flickering in the dark rift of the land that Tom initially had visited.

They all glided through the orbit airspace past the ample comets floating in effervescent colors, like lost dreams wanting to be caught. A thin layer of marshmallow clouds masked the full moon standing bright and proud as if they were guards of the sublime. The moon was so clear white and laden with deep crevices forming potholes and small craters, it appeared like fresh Gouda cheese. The planet dazzled, floating brightly. James, although in awe, remained silent, his eyes wide open and still. They all stood on the banks of Tumblewood in Oblivionarna. The whole place was filled with blue sapphire lights blinking brightly and at rapid speed on the rugged surface beneath. It was as if it the lights were. James suddenly became agitated.

"Look, Iktomi, I didn't come here for this." James was indignant.

"All I came here to do was to rescue Princess Anna-Lisa and take her back to planet Earth with me, where she will be safe away from Morkann." James was not aware of the distance to Moradiya to rescue the princess did not understand that they had landed in Oblivionarna, Tumblewood, with his Mother. Lindiarna was now on her land. She knew the steps of where the good met evil. Although, she was on her land her face was fraught with anxiety, apprehension, and bewilderment. So much had changed, and she now resembled a lost child.

Chapter VI
The Flame of Death

(This chapter contains Latin)

Amber starlight shined mournfully across the horizon suppressing the Milky-Way like a beacon in the cape had pressed against the world, blurring the lines of reality and imagination.

As the area rumbled, a shiver made a muscle jump out of Tom's spine. Tom wandered on, bewildered, toward James and Lindiarna and caught sight of the trickster Iktomi glancing at him, which instantly resulted in the devious Iktomi revealing his intentions. He quickly shot his eyes toward Lindiarna, who returned his gazes with a long gawp. Iktomi's face was watching the strange creature transform was to see the color first melt into a pale shade of sodium, as if to blend into the ground like a chameleon. He then transmuted into the little frail being they had first met. Tom witnessed it. The trickster revealed himself as he truly was.

"You don't seem happy, Lindiarna," Iktomi suggested sarcastically as he squinted his soft nose up at her gaze.

Lindiarna stood like a proud statuesque figure in the distant unforgiving wasteland. The harsh, dusty wind brushed against her body, whipping her face with its sodium-colored haze. This was the stark land she had once left behind. The planet was an ancient cluster that had collided with futuristic horizons forming rocky, sharp spires then sliced the abyss, shooting short florescent flickers of light to float and vanish in to the galactic airspace. These were otherwise known as shooting stars. Lindiarna silently gazed through the floating, vibrant stars onto the forbidden, barren land before her. Tom, still watching Iktomi's intentions, nudged James at his discovery; bewildered, they both stared at the devious character.

"You have changed Iktomi", Lindiarna said.

Smirking, "Yes, I have." Iktomi answered.

"Why did you change"? Lindiarna asked.

"Morkann gave me refuge after your father, King Cepheus died no-one looked after anyone and all the stars were at war. So I changed allegiances".

"But you were treated well, were you not?" asked Lindiarna wearily.

"No-one belongs to anyone and I can do as I wish?" snapped Iktomi.

Iktomi was, scowling at both boys, with his sly, slithery, whining voice spoke. "This was where it was once suggested, when the land was young, that a humongous explosion collided with the future purple horizon, and after much upheaval many planets separated and were formed, causing the beings of that land to be dispersed across the various orbits. This of course created a gorge of dunes and mountainous ridges, all forming openings with rocky canyons. They created large and small ravines with pernicious sand dunes while precious turquoise, shimmering liquid, formed rivulets through its hazardous terrain, dispersing the jewels of turquoise stones and emerald gems shimmering in the ravine."

James was totally aghast at the wilderness before him. He no longer thought of his love, Princess Anna-Lisa. James was completely mesmerized by Iktomi's transformation. All he could do now was watch Iktomi parade in this brutal place, wondering if he could be trusted or not and if they would survive with the great trickster looking after them and being at their side.

Iktomi turned to face the family and hobbled closer to them. He no longer seemed to be frightened of them. He turned to face Lindiarna and proudly spoke. "You may be in your land, Lindiarna, but much has changed; there are now hostile mounds and spirits that lurk in the liquid, languishing in the crevices of the boulders fallen from Moradiya. Temperatia-Morkann is slowly reinstating more power—you realise that, don't you?" he slowly asked Lindiarna, who had become startled.

Lindiarna and James turned to each other. It was obvious that James did not trust Iktomi, how could he? After, all he was a trickster; Iktomi had tried to kill him on their first encounter. James appeared puzzled and very nervous, yet curious about even entertaining such a strange character or would-be friend.

"So Iktomi, why don't I believe that you are going to help us?" James questioned incredulously. Tom watched his older brother glare at Iktomi intently but remained silent.

Iktomi noticed Tom's constant gaze. "You are wise to remain silent, yet you have a question," he said in a slippery voice.

Lindiarna glanced at James. She knew that it would be incredible if James were to trust him. So she paused and gradually lowered her eyes, as if to summon someone higher to help. In that moment, a purple meteor zipped through the orbit at great speed. Everyone looked up into the chasm depth of the airspace. All around them everything was floating or zooming, with different color Nebulas in view. The fire-red Nebula was perhaps the most spectacular of all. Iktomi, quickly realising this as his chance to try and convince the family of his loyalty, threw his limp, pink arm, which seemed to have grown miraculously about two meters longer, around them. He gathered together the perplexed family and moved them quickly toward a broken boulder strewn across the ground.

James, still in disbelief, broke free from the character. "What are you doing?"

Tom straightened up, and Lindiarna suddenly began to feel tightness in her arms. Although she was half listening to the discussion between her boys and Iktomi, she broke away from the group and walked a few steps back from where they were standing. Lindiarna realised that the world she had left behind had changed. It seemed the Lupans were no longer free and there was no sign of Jambalee, the loyal servant to Lindiarna and the amazing Dillyan, Halaconia, with her silver transparent wings or even the great Hakeem. It felt as if their safety net had disappeared.

Lindiarna, lost in thought, gazed around the iridescent orbit she now stood in front of. All that she was able to see were large floating Nebulas in fluorescent colors and strange angular shapes in red, lime, orange, and deep purple all dangling, twinkling, and shining.

Her loyal servant Jambalee appeared, and with him the Unicorn James had saved from certain death and the fearless Halaconia. Both Jambalee and Halaconia smiled as if they had reached their destination. Tom, from the corner of his eye, could see his Mom's relief as the familiar faces grew nearer toward them. Lindiarna's eyes lit up as rivulets of tears dripped from her confused face. She gave a welcome smile and breathed a sigh of relief. A conundrum of thoughts splashed through her mind, darting fragments of her childhood as she reminisced about her past.

Not knowing whether to smile or not to smile, she gazed directly at the strange beings approaching her.

Although it had been many years since Lindiarna had seen Jambalee, she knew instantaneously that it was her loyal servant.

As Jambalee, Halaconia, and the Unicorn approached, it was what Lindiarna had expected. There Jambalee, the little Lupan stood. He was brave, fearless loyal servant in his strange brown coat, which clearly looked too big for him, yet it appeared ageless. The darkness of the surroundings dotted between flickering stars created a kaleidoscope of iridescent colors bouncing off Lindiarna's face and then toward both James's and Tom's faces.

Seeing the Unicorn, James excitedly sprinted to his side, patting and stroking him quite hard, trying to convince him of why he was delayed in his return. James, began to nuzzle him and caress the Unicorns neck. "There, there…it's OK. You're OK now. I'm back." James lovingly patted the Unicorn, whilst caressing and stroking the neck of the slender muscular Unicorn trying to control and reassure him. The beast nuzzled up closely, creating a vibrating sound with his mouth, his almond eyes beaming up at James. It was obvious that the Unicorn had missed his master. James stroked and patted his fur coat. He watched intently as the Unicorn lowered his large, almond-shaped topaz eyes and released a single tear as he nuzzled into James's shoulder. Both Lindiarna and Tom watched intently, knowing that the bond between James and the Unicorn was still very strong, almost unique, and appeared quite remarkable. After much time on caressing his beloved Unicorn, James patted his temple asking the Unicorn,

"Come, show me where the Princess is." James gently pulled the Unicorn's neck toward him, gazing at his silver horn, nuzzling him and patting his neck lovingly.

Tom deliberated, cautiously peering around the purple starlit horizon. He gazed up at his older brother's playful interaction with his beloved Unicorn. He felt it safe that he was also able to stroke the powerful, slender, smooth white coat of the rescued majestic creature. As Tom stepped forward to stroke the creature's neck, he began to wonder and notice the Unicorn's silver horn sparkling in the twilight sky. *Something is not quite right,* he thought. Although the environment was sparse and covered with broken stars and flashing light flares, something was about to happen, and Tom could sense it the Unicorn's horn, confirmed by its shimmering brightly in a carousel of colors. He closed his eyes tightly for a spilt second, turned around swiftly to glance at his Mother, and then walked toward the white muscular Unicorn. Tom's eyes shifted nervously as the Unicorn shuffled and neighed loudly before Tom could grab his neck to guide him into position. Tom, James, and Jambalee quickly glimpsed up at the peculiar, heavy shadow now enveloping the airspace around them. They all squinted and frowned in astonishment, wondering what was happening. Lindiarna scaled the horizon, but she had not lived on the planet for a very long time and so the strange happenings were just more peculiar!

The cloud seemed to be hovering over the luminous, gaseous stars. Iktomi froze, licking his lips, clearly contemplating his next action. It appeared Iktomi was not as anxious as the others. Whilst Jambalee knew something was clearly wrong, he tried to usher both boys and Lindiarna toward a large fracture in the planet that would act as a cave. Jambalee watched cautiously as they all stepped toward the crevice. He peered back at the Unicorn.

"Look! Why is he blowing like that?" Asked Tom anxiously. "What does that mean?"

"When the Unicorn blows like that at something, he usually is curious. I think he is also aware of the Galzar! "said Jambalee a he watched the family with Unicorn.

Lindiarna began to speak to Halaconia in Latin, *"Quod fuerit longum tempus, Ut diu Halaconia fidelis es, qui fuit. Veni abscondam hic nobiscum."* (It has been a long time, Halaconia. You are loyal as ever. Come, you will hide here with us.) Insisted Lindiarna.

Lindiarna greeted her with a big smile and held her hands tightly. Halaconia lowered her eyes in respect to the truthful Queen, as she spoke. Although Halaconia was in awe of Lindiarna, she listened intently. Halaconia began to flap her silver transparent wings, trying to take flight. Yet for the magnetic field around it was too strong and she was unable to take flight. She frowned nervously and looked up at Lindiarna as if asking for her help.

They were all now hiding in the dark, moss-covered crevice strewn with thick strands of green lichen. The vines dripped like fallen tears, beckoning each person who wanted to live to embrace it as a form of survival.

"Zonal," barked James, "that's the ammonia clouds from Jupiter over there?" He pointed excitedly.

Tom then quickly retorted, "You're right, James that's it! And that's because Jupiter has powerful storms!" The brothers turned to each other and said in unison, "Temperatia!" James grinned at Tom, it was that eureka moment they had wanted. James continued his diagnosis of the cloud now covering the tor. "That's the cloud storm, Jambalee, it's her—Morkann!"

"They are always accompanied by those blue-white lightning strikes. The storms are a result of her evil, moist convection in the atmosphere connected to the evaporation and condensation of water. They are the sites of a strong upward motion from the carbonite air, which leads to the formation of bright and dense clouds. These storms form mainly in the belt regions, and they will protect her army before she strikes. The crimson and blue bolts of lightning strikes and sudden golden light flashes you see on the planet Jupiter are more powerful than those you have on your Earth. You are what we call 'Carbonites, Mortals from a planet that does not see right from wrong." said Jambalee.

"Hold on, I wouldn't say we are all like that!" James protested.

"Yes, you are right, my formidable prince; however, there are fewer of you who hold your conviction. Temperatia, or Morkann, is, as you are aware, a phenomenal creature. She has held her wrath since the war with King Cepheus." Jambalee continued with a heavy sigh, peering up at a nervous Tom, who was listening intently.

Lindiarna glanced over at Jambalee, and then she stared at the abyss in front of her. There was no light to be seen, only the frozen white clouds in the form of strangely shaped asteroids floating in an obscure manner. Lindiarna and her sons were now locked in their shadow in a corner of a hidden cave between the planet's crevices.

"There is no life here that meets the eye!" Jambalee retorted, protectively huddling Halaconia and the Unicorn deeper into the cave. "Never allow what you are looking at to determine what you believe, my dear arbonites! Never allow what you can see with your eyes to lure you into the belief that there is nothing more. Alas, allow your spiritual eyes to take you beneath the surface." Jambalee finished his rhyme while gazing deeply at Lindiarna.

James, Tom, and Halaconia felt a presence of cold stillness pour through the cave at that very moment. The sharp wind was biting and nipped at James's and Tom's ears.

"Argh!" Tom shrieked, throwing his hands over his ears to try to stop the icy wind from biting them. His hands turned a bright red.

James too yelled out while trying to bow down to avoid the biting wave. He shook and dropped his shoulders, trying to protect his ears. Grimacing, James tried to stop the Unicorn from jumping up and began to calm him down while watching Tom in pain.

Halaconia could but watch, as her wings were frozen. Upset and agitated, wiping her wings as if to bring them to life, she peered at Jambalee in despair.

"What next? What's happening?" squealed an angry Halaconia, who seemed annoyed at her wings' refusal to come alive.

Jambalee thoughtfully walked over to the void within the clearing of the cove. He looked over at the wispy white Unicorn and the strong teenagers with Lindiarna. "We must enter the terrain before us most prudently, for if not we will come across the chilling, dark galaxies of Galzar."

Lindiarna, listening intently, gazed deeply into Jambalee's eyes. "So what if we try to escape?"

Jambalee gave a half smile and replied assertively, "Then we will undoubtedly fall into the galaxy of Rexorum *(of the kings)* and the entire fury that will accompany it."

Everyone looked stunned at Jambalee's comments. "So - what? Are we going to just sit here and wait for the destruction?" demanded James angrily.

"The Galzarian portal is something we must be conscious of, for it will be our greatest battle yet," insisted Jambalee. "But for now we are trapped on the fringes of Tumblewood." Jambalee paused, glancing around at the milkshake-colored horizon.

Tom peered at him closely. He was after all a strange-looking creature, with his spiky hair and his odd winding pointing hat and a too tightly one buttoned coat. He really was a puzzle.

James stopped stroking his beloved Unicorn while watching Halaconia fiddle with her silver transparent wings.

She was so beautiful, albeit small. James always had a soft spot for her, so he walked over, softly asking, "Do you want some help?"

She peered up at James with her bright, wide-open gazelle shaped amber eyes, fluttering her eyelashes like a cartoon character. "Not sure what you will be able to do, but go on. Thank you," she replied, releasing her hold on her silver wings. James held the silver wing. It felt heavy and tired. He began to gently massage her wing. Halaconia began to scrutinize James's action and smiled nervously. She knew James was once smitten with her, despite her wings.

He released the wing back to her. "Take this," said James, smiling anxiously.

"James, I can feel my wing—"

Before she could continue, the Unicorn jolted, jumping up on his hind legs and neighing loudly. Lindiarna and Jambalee gazed cautiously through the cove further from where they were all hiding inside. There was a dull rush and gush sound of liquid. As they both peered, they could see an inky sapphire-blue ocean surge and swell, and it was heading toward the cave.

"Quick! We all have to get out of here now. The war is imminent. Morkann's ghouls will attack from the edge of the Mountains of the Moon!" Jambalee roared. They, Jambalee and James took a breath, looking at each other with wide-open eyes. There was a short silence, enough to contemplate who was now waging their wrath. James grabbed Halaconia by her petit hand and told her to embark on the Unicorn, while

Jambalee navigated a way out of the cove without being hit by Temperatia's ocean storm that was heading their way.

The Unicorn again jolted and then unexpectedly blew, his horn then started to glisten and shimmer in a dazzling silver-white light. It was effervescent and appeared holy. Both James and Tom were amazed.

All that was now visible beneath the surface of the terrain they stood upon was a dark, eerie shadow languishing in obscure shapes, and then there it was: the towering rage of blue-white Sulphur tide, slashing the jagged rock of the cove.

"Look— out!" howled Tom to anyone who was near. There was sudden madness with everyone running in the small space. As the Unicorn jumped out of the cave and into the air, his horn once again twinkled with a luminous orange tone. Halaconia was still sat on the Unicorn's back, hanging on for her life and trying aimlessly to free her wings from their discomfort. "Argh!" Tom grabbed the Unicorn by his long, white-silver tail, quickly clambering on as they moved slowly through the strange, surreal galactic landscape. Tom could see clearly a blue-green sky punctured by broken stars shimmering in the dark void of deep space. James, Lindiarna and Jambalee were caught up in the stillness of the magical surrounding. A gush of sapphire-green ocean froze over into a cotton-wool sky as the comets danced and bounced off the edge of Tumblewood.

The whole episode took only but a few moments, however, it felt like hours had passed. Lindiarna turned to Jambalee for reassurance.

"I thought we were in Tumblewood," she said restlessly.

"We are! Much has changed, Lindiarna, much has changed!" Jambalee replied with a gloomy visage, and then he let out a sigh of sorrow.

"What is it, Jambalee? What has happened?" Lindiarna

"When the poison for King Cepheus was administered, many Lupans, Dillyans and Orags, and other beings were astonished that the poison of radiation took so long to take hold. We knew and when the shaman tried to intervene he was changed to stone!" Lindiarna gasped in disbelief and horror. "It was a slow death, one that should not have been visible to any eye."

Chapter VII
The Journey

Jambalee glanced around the deep labyrinth into the cove and noticed Iktomi was not there. "Where is Iktomi?" he said. Turning to Lindiarna, he asked, "Lindiarna, Where did he get to?"

Lindiarna gawped, her eyes now wide open in horror, still trying to overcome her great sadness of her father the death of King Cepheus. She felt she was being subjected to a conundrum of possibilities. She levitated over toward the roaring waves surging into the cave. The gales began to slap her auburn hair, causing it to fall across her face. Squeezing her eyes tightly she looked at Jambalee. They both became frightened at what Iktomi appeared to be planning.

"I don't know where he is. He will turn up, I am sure." she answered

Jambalee, with a puzzled look, gazed out from the cave anxiously in search of Iktomi, "He has changed," Jambalee insisted, referring to Iktomi as he slid past the blushing

133

acid stream. Lindiarna, resigned to the fact that Iktomi had disappeared and was nowhere to be seen, she was disarray and alarmed that the creature could trick her and indeed her son.

Jambalee understood that he was right all along. "James, you were right. I am sorry I did not believe you," Jambalee said. "Iktomi is a foolish trickster, his lie does not become truth or right. His evil must not be allowed to become righteous, and he must not be trusted - yet." Jambalee was really infuriated and upset that he had not believed the son of Lindiarna. Then he spotted the abhorrent creature. "Quick—there he is." Jambalee bellowed pointing to the large swooping wave heading toward the cave, as the angry, rapid wave trampled onto the ledge of the cave. The waves rushed in thrusting its overpowering and forceful wind commandeering the Sulphur waves that swirled against the comets strewn around the terrain. Natalya, Halaconia, Tom and James along with Lindiarna all huddled together. The tempest was enraged, and Morkann's wrath had commenced.

James stared at the large, angry, grey wave battling across the tor toward the cave. "That's it?" James shook his head. "You see, the darkness…these are the shards of cacophony! I told you there was something not right with that creature!" Jambalee bellowed defiantly, his voice simply echoing around the rocks in the cave.

James stood tall, his muscular arms protruding out of his tight T-shirt, the water drizzled from the oncoming wave, and with his dust-streaked, faded Levis, the length of his legs was now apparent. His wet blue jeans contoured around his body. He was a handsome young man, towering over his Mom and Jambalee. James dipped his eyebrows and let out a deep sigh. He always knew that Iktomi had many faces, he was not called the trickster for nothing.

James turned to face Jambalee. "Now what shall we do?" James questioned doubtfully.

Iktomi, walked toward the family stranded in the cave. The wave drenched the ground and everything was water logged.

Jambalee, unhappy with Iktomi and his troublemaking behavior toward Lindiarna and her sons, began to think of something to make Iktomi aware of his actions. The malevolent creature had clearly transformed into a wild torrent, aiding Morkann with his deception of his wish to switch sides between the wicked Temperatia and the righteous, gentle Lindiarna.

Then the ground suddenly gave way beneath where James was standing. After a tumultuous groan in the surround, stars were seen shooting rapidly in every direction, "James! Look out! Shouted Jambalee, as Tom rushed deeper into the cave. It was too late, he fell into a deep, pulverized rock that began to slowly swallow him up.

James yelled, "Argh, what's going on? What's happening?" His face stretched with anxiety.

135

He turned to face Jambalee. "What now?" James questioned doubtfully.

"James grab onto something!" bellowed Natalya.

"James, you will have to take hold of something, I will try and throw you a vine". Jambalee bellowed as Tom looked on.

"Tom, give me the potion pot – now!" shouted Natalya to a apprehensive Tom, as he quickly wrenched the pot out of his rucksack. Jambalee began to heave a loose vine hanging from the cave to throw to James.

As Jambalee began to throw the vine, across to James, Natalya quickly threw some drops of the potion from the pot.

The ground slowly whirled round into a frenzy, like a washing machine on its last cycle. Lindiarna was aghast in sheer horror. She deliberated her next move. She drew her strength and was able to take flight in order to snatch back her son, but James was injured and as he took one step, he fell back into the sinkhole. The drops from the potion pot had not worked as well as they should have. Distraught, he glared at his Mom and Jambalee,

"Help me!" he screamed in agony. The hideous squelching sound of James squirming and sinking into the thick quicksand, spurred a tumultuous rupture and a large sinkhole appeared. The rubble fell bouncing off the comets and galactic airspace around them. Everyone gasped in horror. "Quick Natalya, pass me the vine we have to get him out!" yelled Lindiarna. Tom then threw the vine

Natalya had found to James and they all heaved, pulling on the vine with all their might as Lindiarna's tears fell, only to sMother her silky face like a veil of love. Her determination showed in how she tried to pull her older son out of the quicksand then away from the sinkhole.

'Help me! He screamed. Lindiarna heaved with all her might, as her tears fell only to smother her silky face like a veil of love.

His face was streaked with blood and sweat as James struggled to hold onto the vine, his grip was slipping so Lindiarna tried to pass out her arm to him. He groaned in pain. The moment intensified and felt like an avalanche. Jambalee quickly began to pull at his coat pocket in search for some of his magic potion powder. Unable to retrieve any of the potions Tom quickly handed some of the potion to Jambalee.

He rapidly threw some of the potion from the pouch, that Tom had given him into the sinkhole, watching every white grain cascade and evaporate into nothing until it quickly disappeared.

"Here, take this, James, you going to be OK!" Tom said.

The sinkhole simply vanished as if it had melted away, disintegrating into nothing like snow from a fire, and its place in the ground only appeared bruised and burnt. James watched on shaking from his ordeal and although in shock and injured Jambalee continued sprinkling some of the magic potion into the galactic airspace.

He then walked back toward the entrance of the cave, still nursing his wounds. The Milky-Way horizon unexpectedly turned deep red, this was a clear sign that blood had been shed or it was to be be shed, somewhere at that very moment.

James watched the horizon, as he could see in the distance the streaks of crimson lava soar widely into the galactic airspace as an erupting volcano displayed the most spectacular light show in vivid iridescent colors.

Temperatia was known for her malevolent nature, and so she threw blinding angry flashes of explosive forked lightening, solar flares and dancing nebulas, which cracked the red-hot sky to show just the sort of fireworks she had at her command. The hot ash golden particles dispersed across the loose ground, burning everything that they fell on to.

James and Lindiarna grimaced at the display of fireworks. Fixated on what they were now in view of. James although in pain, was relieved he came out the sink hole alive. They all stood still, their eyes locked like flashbulbs and were unable to blink. Jambalee swiftly turned to face Lindiarna and then quickly back to James, who was injured and still nursing his arm.

Although, both James and Lindiarna appeared distraught and angry at Temperatia's evil wrath, they continued to examine their injuries while very carefully trying to peep out of the cave. They noticed that a sudden surge of angry grey waves coming toward them had ceased and James was able to see the rocky lava ground, still bruised and burnt but clearly where once the sinkhole had appeared.

He was totally mystified about the large sinkhole vanishing and at Jambalee's astonishing control of the impending giant waves, as well as the sudden crimson lightning strikes. Look like Iktomi has disappeared again, said Halaconia as she nursed her wings.

"He will be back, when of course he is not wanted". Natalya replied.

The surrounding tor had become drenched with thick green swinging lichen, flowing due to the heavy precipitation from the waves following the sudden roaring of Temperatia's gush of waves.

All of these strange happenings drew him closer to the strange Lupan, Jambalee.

Lindiarna turned to face her loyal and humble servant, Jambalee. Her lips parted gently as she began to utter the words he longed to hear. "Jambalee, I am so glad you were here to help us. Please tell me, when did my father, King Cepheus, leave and go to the other world?" Lindiarna asked weeping.

Jambalee took in a deep gulp of carbon, his eyes drooped woefully, and he raised his eyebrows, trying to remain still as a statue. He grasped Lindiarna's arm tersely and yelled out, "Lindiarna, it was after the battle of Typhoona! This was when the doors of death opened, and you were still in the Carbonite world. This proved it was all too much for our dear King Cepheus. This my child took its toll on our good King Cepheus. Alas, he was no longer able to sustain the torment of the open doors of death or indeed of you becoming a Carbonite." Jambalee moaned pausing and wandering around like an old, strict headmaster.

Lindiarna's muscles in her svelte throat slowly began to constrict as she lowered her eyes and drops of silver diamonds fell. Whispering tentatively and as soft as silk, she repeated her words, swallowing to try to absorb the inevitable words she had dreaded to say or hear. "The Carbonite world is where he said I should go to be safe from the wrath of Morkann! You do know that, Jambalee? For so many years, I have been torn between two wants: living in the Carbon world, you know as planet Earth with my carbon, mortal family and of course returning to my planet with my father. I spent years on that planet existing as a mere Carbonite, absorbing the mortal realities. But now she has taken everything. I do not seek retribution, Jambalee, for revenge is the way of darkness. I know that without shedding one tear nothing is ever clear, Jambalee!"

Lindiarna was distraught, her tears fell like a veil, covering her face. Her father had died, and she now was to be the new Queen. Jambalee held Lindiarna's hand, trying to console her.

"My Queen, Morkann has destroyed our very existence. We cannot continue as servants to the demon Queen Morkann. If we do, - we will perish. She has cleared the pathway to get to you directly. She will make it difficult for you, and only the loyal and the strong can save you now. Alas, it is we and the Lupan army who are with you Lindiarna." Natalya said hesitantly as she walked up close to both Jambalee and Lindiarna.

Lindiarna stared deep into the surrounding tor, her eyes fixated without a single blink as her green eyes transformed into diamond stones. "I seek peace and must not thwart in abundance. This is my galaxy, my land, and my people. There is no justice. I cannot just let her succeed. She must be stopped in her quest!"

Natalya knew of Lindiarna's forthcoming peril and she stopped in her speech, watching the doomed Lindiarna. "Lindiarna, the prophecy has been written you will be strong. I am here with you to guide you out of the maze. I will take you and your sons to the beginning of the labyrinth, where I will be able to give the route to achieve final victory."

She gave a nervous smile to Natalya then momentarily stared intently at Jambalee, knowing of her impending fate. Her tears had ceased, frozen in their escape from her glacier eyes; now Lindiarna was a defiant creature and had become strong once again.

Lindiarna paused and raised her head, her eyes now heavily waterlogged and bulging as the tears ran down her face. Once she had comprehended the state of her pending battle with Morkann, she realised she would have to take her natural state and was obliged to surrender her current display so that she could obtain the image that would turn her into Queen Lindiarna. She precipitously felt her power suddenly become resilient and steadfast.

"My father, King Cepheus, would not have wanted me to hide away from the planets in fear. He would not want me to disappear into the Carbon world. The time has now arrived! Jambalee, I must fight this battle! I cannot have war without an end, and this must end! I must win for my dear father, King Cepheus, and for my dear, dear Oblivionarna."

Jambalee smiled in relief. "My Queen. Do not be frightened – this is your fate." he said graciously.

Lindiarna continued tersely. "You will tell me when the time arrives for me to relinquish all ties with the Carbon World."

Jambalee knew Lindiarna was now ready to become the power of Oblivionarna once again. She had returned, and she understood what was to become of her if or when she would return to the land. The power that once had been neglected for so long would return with a vengeance for all to see. Watching closely, he scrutinized his Princess and spoke pithily. "You will take my advice, dear Princess, and you will once again become our princess—Princess Lindiarna!" Jambalee dipped his head and sunk his lips close to his chest, giving out a deep sigh of liberation.

James, who was standing nearby, listened and watched intently as the obscure custom unfolded before him. He was witnessing something that perhaps he should not have been privy to. What he saw was the transformation of his Mother into an unseen creature. Lindiarna transformed into an angelic figurine from the splinters of motes floating in abundance around them. Through, the wild rhythm, chanting and thumping of rocks, Lindiarna was to relinquish herself as a mortal.

Her skin appeared like a porcelain doll, her Auburn hair bright, emulating the soleus at when the mortal world is in slumber. Her diamond glacier eyes were once more emerald, shiny, bright, and transparent. She had now metamorphosed into an angelic being. Her celestial form levitated to a higher majestic scale. Her hands transformed into silk, slight and airy. She was wrapped in a golden transparent emblem of bright white light. James, trying hard to keep his eyes open so as to witness the transformation, was forced to cover his eyes, as the light was blinding, too luminous. He scrunched his eyes tightly, trying to hold back the bright light fighting its way into his eyes.

He tried to peek through, yet he was unable to distinguish the symbols dotted on her long white gown, which suddenly appeared as her new apparel. She looked something like what could quite easily have been read in a storybook.

"What's going on? Is she dead? Mom?" he questioned, hoping Jambalee would answer. But he did not. James became puzzled and distraught. "What's happening? Why is she changing?" James asked perplexed at his Mothers' change.

But his voice was not heard, and with his teary eyes, he glared intensely at his Mom. James very quickly began to realize what had just befallen right in front of him "Behold! I tell you a mystery. You shall not all sleep, but you shall be changed, in a moment, in the twinkling of an eye, at the last trumpet. For the trumpet will sound, and the light will be raised imperishable. Then for this perishable body must put on the imperishable, and this mortal body must put on immortality. When the perishable puts on the imperishable, and the mortal puts on immortality, then shall come to pass the saying that is written: *"Death is swallowed up in victory .O death, where is your victory? O death, where is your sting?"* The words reiterated by Jambalee confirmed Lindiarna's mortal image was to fade in death and on its place she now appeared as an image of light. James eyes darted in every direction, trying to comprehend he had been witnessing the death of his Mother? Lindiarna, in the image he had seen all his life, had changed in front of him. She had now become Queen Lindiarna of Oblivionarna, returning to her land. But she would have to forfeit her life as a Carbonite to rejoin the dominion lands.

He sighed, only to release a single silver tear, which silently crept down his rugged, young bone structure, but his eyes remained wide open. He stood still as a statue, unable to do anything, frozen as in fear of fear itself.

Before the glistening silver tear hit the ground, Lindiarna realising James had witnessed all of what had occurred, held out her arm, stretching her hand, and seized his tear, gripping it tightly into her palm. Turning to James, she said, "My son, you will not shed a mortal tear of sadness, I am still your Mother! Though the mountains be stolen and the hills be removed, yet my unfailing love for you will not be shaken nor my covenant of peace be removed! Remember this, my son!"

Still holding the tear, Lindiarna blew into it as if a magician was to conduct a spectacle, and it dispersed into a thousand pieces like a fountain into the atmosphere. Lowering her soft eyes, she closed them and gently released a puff of air through her tightly closed lips.

James was stunned at Lindiarna's transformation of the tear into tiny silver diamond droplets that was cast among a plume of white smoke emerging softly. James looked on, marveling at the vision and at the many traits his Mother possessed. Yet, he was perplexed, almost bemused at the same time, fearful of her transformation and now her apparent magic. Lindiarna gave a soft smile, and as if by magic itself created a chain from nowhere as if plucked out of the stars, she placed the newly created dazzling diamond around the neck of her son. What is going on, he wondered to himself, among the many distorted thoughts lurking and roaming through his mind. Completely befuddled at that very moment, he pondered, Who is this woman? Creature? Alien? Is she my Mother? Oh, this is crazy! So many thoughts just darted through his young mind, all with their unique color, zooming and whizzing from one thought to another.

Jambalee was not afraid. He took Lindiarna's svelte soft hand, and in a subservient manner, gave her the Shield of Life along with his scabbard encrusted with rubies and topazes, all glistening and fighting to escape the heavy golden case. "You must take this, my Queen!" Jambalee bellowed as he handed her the heavy weapon.

Lindiarna grasped the sword, a bright light from the sword beamed a kaleidoscope of colors, illumining each encrusted jewel set. Ensuring that even the stars would dance, the light from the splinters of ruby jewels were like dreams scattered from an angel's wing, only to be dispersed across each carbon soul, leaving fragments of wishes to immerse for more.

James was aghast and gave a shallow smile of contentment about what he was witnessing. Even a dream could not be so beautiful, he thought to himself. James understood that his Mother had finally returned home.

Jambalee Lindiarna felt it necessary to advise of Morkann's new power. "Lindiarna, Queen, oh Queen, you must defeat Temperatia!" Jambalee begged. "For she and only she possess the evil energy from every individual from the Carbon world that you leave. For you know her wrath is danger beyond danger, and her hair is riddled with strands of the darkest slithering serpents, praying for its new kill. Her malicious hands, with her withered fingers, tired of the poison she carries, bears no power except for herself. Be warned that it is her tongue, her green tongue has no bones, yet it is so strong—strong enough to break the blackest of hearts like glass! Her wrath is of envy and venom. You, Queen, oh dearest Queen, you have the power to dampen her, to remove her from her quest! Lindiarna, you must know of this!" Jambalee was so obstinate that he could advise Lindiarna of Morkann's devilish traits.

Lindiarna listened intently, her trembling lips and trembling body now in anticipation of the new world before her. She opened her eyes wide, still in horror as to what Jambalee had warned her of. She seemed to comprehend everything. She was no longer a suburban Mother once found on Earth, for she now was a Queen in a dominion land on a planet. Jambalee had said the words required to eradicate her of any human form. She was floating in a celestial screen of light smothered in a golden aura. Lindiarna had been transformed into a Queen, losing all sight of the Carbon Mother of Earth. She tentatively began to repeat the words of Jambalee's recital of the oath she would have to honor as the new Queen. Lindiarna held the book of Oracles, and whilst holding the encrusted book, repeated each word tentatively.

147

I bestow upon you;-

I tell you I am your Queen!

I am the new valiant Sovereign.

I seek the Dominion lands, which you have seen.

I seek no retribution or be mean; I must not devour the
sacred code.

But live in an abode of love.

That, which no one has seen.

I promise to uphold from the sinews of my heart,

To be the loyal Queen for the Kingdom and to be kind,
and obedient to the beings and creatures I find on my
land.

For the Temperatia, the wrath will not rule our land.

She will disappear—this is my quest, I found.

Of a land unseen. I stand with my beings so that
Moradiya will not return to sand.

I will not let Temperatia gain any stand.

The valiant Queen, the stars and comets are my jewels
in my crown,

The beings that live with me are for now my real destiny.

Lindiarna shared her rights and obligations, she knew
only too well that the destiny of a great kingdom rested
upon her shoulders.

The gravity and pride of her homecoming felt too large
to absorb. After, she willingly repeated each verse slowly
and concisely, Jambalee read each line to her one by one,

the rights of her decree. She continued to place her hand onto the book of Oracles and watched it shimmer when each verse was read. Finally, the declaration had ended and Lindiarna looked at Jambalee knowing that she would slowly leave her life form.

Jambalee gave a half smile of assurance and then turned suddenly to face James, whose face was in turmoil. His eyes were open wide, locked and frozen in apprehension. His breathing became labored as he gawped at Jambalee. James had witnessed his Mother change into a celestial creature, into a beam of golden light, a hologram, she, no longer had the visible a human image appearance like him. But then he could not help but contemplate whether he too would transform into a light source. This fear and anxiety was etched upon his face, burning at his very soul. Turning to Jambalee with a deep frown, James's face dropped.

"Is she dead?" James asked as he watched the glistening light flicker.

Jambalee began to reassure him, "James, remember the righteous never dies and is always close to the brokenhearted, he will rescue those whose spirits are crushed. You and your brother are from the Carbon planet and are mortals, you will not see what is found between the crevices of our planet. Now you wear the diamond of eternal life, bestowed by your Mother, our Queen, Lindiarna. Be sure your tear will not fall in vain, for this diamond tear you wear around your neck will warn you of the dangers you will face. James, you are the firstborn son of Lindiarna, Queen of Oblivionarna".

James crumbled as he absorbed the potent words Jambalee released.

Lindiarna, stood tall and beamed her bright light at her son. "Mom, you can see me – right?"

"Yes, my son I can see you." Replied a broken Lindiarna, her voice as soft as silk, but her words carried the whole size of the cave. Tom and James were now in awe of their Mother.

Jambalee, walked over to Lindiarna and took the book of Oracles from her before Natalya, Tom with Halaconia walked over toward them, but Iktomi, who was lurking behind the rock crevice suddenly appeared having silently watched the transformation of Lindiarna take place. This was the time, he felt to take his role and snatch the royal throne from Lindiarna as she was weak and alone and away from Morkann.

"Mom, what happened to you? Why are you shining like that?" Tom asked inquisitively. Natalya could see the transformation and knew instantly his Mother a beam of light was the indication of her forfeit her life to return home.

Iktomi marched over proudly in his red robe and staring at Tom he blurted "Child, your Mother is dead!"

Tom wide eyed and in shock was pulled back from a angry Natalya. James and Halaconia came to his rescue.

"What do you mean Dead! I mean Mom is not really, I still see her through th light – yes." Tom snapped.

Iktomi, snarled and glared at Jambalee, "You Jambalee, have served the realm long and faithfully, and every creature in Oblivionarna owes you thanks. Yet, now I fear your service is at an end. This is the wish of my Queen and…"

"Your Queen, the Demon Queen who holds malice and distrust!" Natalya Interrupted.

Chapter VIII
The Wrath of War

The war was near, and had commenced. Jambalee could see the soldiers lining up for the battle, below the Mountain of the Moon in Moradiya. This was Morkann territory and everything was absorbed in a dark evil hue. There were many Lupans line up with Centaurs all led by Aspero, who was proudly mounted on his strong, fierce creature resembling a horse, Ara. Aspero was a tall, muscular powerful figure. He was lean, with a ramrod-straight back and a precisely angled, rock-hard jaw, as if it had been chiseled. He had broad shoulders that seemed mitered at perfect ninety-degree angles. He mouth was narrow and long and seemed like a jigsaw piece had to fit into his face. He was the Lupan leader, the brave one, and indeed a strong warrior, to whom the beautiful Halaconia was betrothed. Aspero was of an olive complexion and possessed a jagged bone structure. His face was ridged and powerful, and his gunmetal eyes were bold and bright. Although they appeared like gunmetal close up, they looked purple from a distance. His raccoon eyes were framed with dark, angular eyebrows. He wore his long sleek black hair poker straight, tied back into a ponytail that flopped like a pencil down his back. He wore dark symbolic markings of a strange code on his strong, well-developed torso, illustrating his strength and power. The muscles of his arms protruded through his skin, indicating his dominance and endurance. Each vein was visible, humanlike, but he wasn't human, or even a Carbonite.

Chiron, the Centaur, had taken position with their creatures behind the Valley of Doom. Each Centaur was a valiant creature in the battlefield including Chiron and Aspero needed him with the rest of the Centaurs to help win their battle against Morkann's deadly ghouls. However, he knew, only too well the only way to win the conflict once and for all was to eliminate and destroy Morkann, the demon princess.

Aspero embarks on his mission to win against Morkann's Ghouls.
The strong powerful Aspero leads in the battlefield with his horse Ara.

Tom observed, closely watching the peculiar habits of this powerful creature. He became nauseated while gazing at Aspero and the many odd creatures lining up for battle. He was totally captivated and in awe of Aspero's strength and control yet feeling somehow insecure in his presence.

The battle commenced, and the ghouls were dark, malevolent creatures, with thin skin and gaunt complexions. Their dark, hollow eyes and protruding teeth, like a crocodile's, were frightening enough to scare even the stars into dimming.

The centaurs slashed the ghouls with their sharp blades and rotating spokes covered with thin, scissor-sharp daggers. The blood or liquid oozed out of the strange creatures as they fell before disintegrating into corpses like burned rag dolls shrinking into particles of dust.

Aspero was sure he would win the battle. He glared intently at the horizon, surveying the battle ground with his sharp purple eyes. The Lupan leader sported clothing like that of a warrior, although minimal. His strength was paramount. He wore an arm bracelet wrapped just below his shoulder, signifying his rank and loyalty to the Lupan army. His broad feet were adorned with leather sandals tied together with brown leather straps swirled around the calf.

The flat sole to his feet stood on a sandal base which appeared to be the hide from a hunted beast. His forearm was covered with a titanium plate that displayed a coded engraving similar to the ones appearing on his chest. Around his waist he wore a long loin cloth that fell almost to his knees. Across the right side of his shoulder to his chest, he had his sword in the diamond-encrusted scabbard, and on his back he wore his titanium shield. He was a powerful warrior—fierce and fearless.

"Aspero, you must go with the others and find Princess Anna-Lisa before Morkann ends her light. The end is near; she will test your very presence. The enemy will never let you rule your land. Iktomi, the trickster is accompanying Morkann, and there is bound to be more disastrous battles ahead. The princess is held in the Mountains of the Moon in Moradiya. We cannot achieve victory if we do not disperse across the lands. We must disperse!" Jambalee instructed.

Aspero frowned but bowed and nodded in agreement.

Tom watched the events unfold before him and felt it was surreal, but he wanted to assist. "I will ride with you," he said.

They all stared back at Tom, who was waiting like a lost child. Lindiarna could now only watch through her golden glow, for she was no longer in human form. She closed her eyes as swiftly as a deer and then glided toward the area where James was about to take flight with his Unicorn.

Everyone was still watching Tom as he shifted uneasily toward Aspero. "Well, I am his brother," Tom insisted, interrupting sharply. Unsure of his actions, Tom felt a sudden panic grip his throat. Swallowing hard, he turned to his Mother for support, but she was quiet as a shadow, still smoldering in her golden glow. He bit his top lip and held his tongue.

Jambalee laughed. "Yes, indeed you are, dear sir." He turned to Tom and then quickly to Aspero. "Take him with you, and give him the king's sword," instructed Jambalee.

Aspero wavered but agreed to the request. He nodded, raising a single dark eyebrow, as he was still unsure of the Carbonite, Tom, having to accompany him and his army on their hazardous journey ahead. He bowed to Queen Lindiarna once more in respect. Lindiarna in turn gave a soft smile through her veil of golden light. Tom turned toward Aspero, guiding him toward Chiron and the army of Centaurs.

"So Aspero, will we go to the Mountains of the Moon? Are you going to rescue her?" asked Tom. He looked at him, with a deep glare, "You want me to save her?" he said disembarking his strong horse. "Well, yes... that is It's James actually, I am not really concerned". Tom protested.

Aspero, smiled at Tom

Aspero was a proud, sharp-faced, flat-browed, regal captain. As Lupan leader, he possessed the required intelligence and bravery for war. In this role he had developed a painstaking special code, a language, which he had memorized before he would train his soldiers.

The language of warriors employed was of course Lupanium.

No one would be able to crack the code, for no one knew how to speak the language, except a select few who were the chosen ones from within the Lupan army. These creatures were all controlled by Aspero.

"I can see the Ghouls; they are mounting up!" said Chiron. He was on the lookout for their fate at the Oracle.

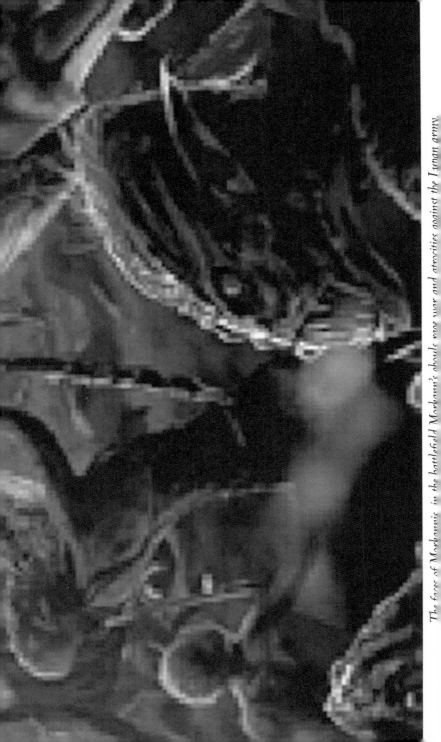

The face of Morkannis in the battlefield. Morkannis's ghouls rage war and atrocities against the Lunan army.

Chiron the Centaur was the powerful, muscular creature who worked alongside Aspero. The mythological creature was the only immortal centaur, with his strong, bare human torso protruding proudly as he stood prominently on his hooves. His eyes were amber shaped and the color of the ocean. His muscles and veins displayed his power. Chiron shook his human head, throwing his long, shiny, black mane over his shoulders. His arms, all bare and robust, were muscular in shape and toned for strength. The remaining body of Chiron was horse, including four legs and hindquarters. Leading his army was his destiny.

He beckoned worrisomely. "I tell you that beyond the stars of time they are mounting up. We must seek the path of right." He moaned apprehensively, pointing with his strong hand into the distance while gazing worriedly with his sharp ocean eyes directly into the double purple moon hiding in the galactic airspace. Chiron and the Lupan army served boldly, with honor distinction, and without fear. The Lupan army was not aggressive but humble and proud, respecting their battalion for the preservation of their land. The battalion stood strong, and although each creature was nervous, no one spoke of any anxiety. Such was the bravery of the Lupan army. Aspero paraded his army, acknowledging their strength. Their actions were to prove critical in sustaining power after the death of their King Cepheus and of course to keep the demon Morkann and her army of ghouls at bay.

Chiron, the lead Centaur helps in the battlefield against Morkann's Ghouls.

"Procrastination is the thief of time—collar him!" they would shout.

As Lupan leader, he possessed the required intelligence and bravery for war. In this role, he had developed a painstaking special code, a language, which he had memorized before he would train his soldiers.

They endured some of the most ferocious battles in the galactic airspace and remained calm in battle.

They all served proudly. King Cepheus had died to keep Morkann and her army of Ghouls at bay.

James looked on and held his Unicorn gently by his neck, caressing it lovingly. He stroked the white glossy mane that draped over the Unicorn's neck like a scarf. The Unicorn gazed obliviously to all that was happening around him, nuzzling into James for comfort he so longed for. Suddenly blue and grey angry waves roared, splashing like white rock salt everywhere bouncing off each comet and boulder in abound. They were like wild mini avalanches from the cobalt rocks, slamming and bashing onto the boulders and comets on the ground. Some waves were high and violent, while some were fierce and some were without an end.

James took in a deep breath, holding onto his Unicorn tightly until he noticed that the tyrant waves suddenly spiraled out of control, splashing and swirling their silver stream in an abrupt gale force wind. Precipitation had all but ceased. It was quite ironic that everything seemed to suddenly stop; not even a drop of silver or salt covered the water that fell, and only a cold chill from nowhere seemed to be moving. James patted his Unicorn leading him onto the dry ash.

Lindiarna, Queen Lindiarna, appeared totally unrecognizable. Her hair transformed into luminous, golden, long, falling, silk tresses; she wore strange apparel in silver, if not white, that did not shimmer but did sparkle when she moved. She appeared saintly. James watched his Mother, who had transformed into something unknown. For this young man, she did not resemble the woman, he would call Mom, he had initially brought with him.

James struggled to understand exactly why she had changed in every way. Why was she adorned, and why she had become light? He could see a strange, illuminating golden glow around her. Gazing hard at the figure he now saw before him, he tried to fathom what the symbols represented on her robe, but he was unable to identify them. James, mesmerized by his Mother's appearance, stared directly into her eyes, noticing that they had changed into a bright diamond opaque color that dazzled James. He was totally perplexed about his Mother's transformation and watched her every move closely. 'Is she alive?' he wondered. His eyes narrowed as he shook his head in hopelessness. He became quite still and his cheek-bones were high and prominent; and his jaws were so long and lank, that an observer would have supposed that he was drawing the flesh of his face in, for a moment, by some contraction of the muscles, if his half-opened mouth and immovable expression had not announced that it was his ordinary appearances he would have struggled to understand what had now become of his Mother.

"Come; we must leave while it is clear," Jambalee suggested, sounding pressured at the thought of Morkann with her sinister army of ghouls or even Iktomi reappearing quickly.

"Yeah, well, what about my mom? And the others, Tom and Halaconia—where are they?" asked James anxiously. He was still lost in deep curiosity about his Mother's appearance.

"Yes, they will all be waiting for us once we leave this place and head for Moradiya—"

James interrupted Jambalee as he ambled cautiously over the gray ash ground, which looked like volcanic debris. "And my Mother? Tell me what has happened to her—tell me!" James insisted, frowning, with fresh tears in his eyes.

"My prince, you are brave, for that there is no doubt. This is a quality to be admired. Yet you are new to our ways and culture in these lands. And you have seen the vision of light in front of your very eyes. "Jambalee paused; a cold silence gripped both him and James. Jambalee realised what his Mother had done, but how would he tell his beloved

James of the plight his Mother had now undertaken? They slowly turned to face each other, appearing stunned that they both knew what had happened to Lindiarna. James, needed one more confirmation. With a distraught look, and water logged eyes, James sought confirmation that his Mother was now dead. How could not he let his mind tell him that his Mother was no more. He glared at Jambalee in the hope that none of what he felt was real. Jambalee placed his arm on the tall figure.

"James, you are a Carbonite; your Mother is not. You must be strong. James, you must not be ignorant about those who fall asleep, or to grieve like the rest of the carbonite men, who have no hope. Your Mother is now the light that will guide you. Trust in the almighty". "James, do not weep, do not put out the Spirits fire; she has now returned to her true self. You know that, don't you?" He consoled James as he absorbed the enormity that his Mother had died on her return to the land but was to appear only as the light source beam he now saw.

James took a deep breath through his nose and continued as if nothing had happened. "You were talking about Jupiter's wands, right?" he said stiflingly, trying to hide his feelings and failing miserably.

"James, you don't need…'" Jambalee said interrupting James from continuing his conversation.

"Yes, those are the wands of change. We will see which wand we will receive," replied Jambalee cautiously, trying to support James. "Our time has now arrived for change. Come!"

Jambalee, although small in stature, was a leader with a mighty voice and presence when he needed to be heard.

Apart from being a loyal servant to Princess Lindiarna, he knew when change was to occur and when he would have to set the seed to disperse into a new era. Peering over at James, he began to speak in an authoritarian voice, commanding the tall, handsome James to follow him through the dense, ash-covered terrain. Tom looked on, "Good luck, James. I will see you on the other side" said Tom

James rolled up the sleeves of his now drenched white shirt, which appeared more gray than white. It seemed old and worn, as did his blue jeans. Jambalee directed James toward a blue light from the illuminating sphere in the distance. Although there was no wind and everything was still and motionless, it was possible to see sporadic shooting stars zooming intermittently whilst flashing by and the flickering of sporadic sky lights, which appeared to display a coded message of something, whispering gentle messages. James could feel the words being etched through the bright sky lights. Lindiarna hovered in a spectrum of bright golden light, guiding them through to Tumblewood to meet the Zonal. The wands of Jupiter were transparent green wafts of mist that revolved around the planet. It was now apparent to James that his Mother's humanoid form had disappeared only to be replaced by the beam of light surrounded by a golden glow. Jambalee was right. She was no more. He did not feel any remorse or sadness, just a void of warmth that his Mother was now in a shield. It was angelic emblem.

They trudged on aimlessly through the dusty terrain across the strange sphere. Lindiarna was guiding them through the strange land using her beam of light. It really did emulate a desert, except there were no palm trees or cacti. The golden, simmering light reflected from Lindiarna's light source shimmered on the gray ash ground slithering like a snake moving, wafting in different directions as if waiting for its prey to rear its ugly head. As they placed one foot in front of the other, they sent wild grains of sand into the abysmal black sky. It seemed like the black space was waiting for the grains of ash to shoot into its kingdom so that it would be able to sparkle just for that split second. After a short distance, which inevitably felt like a lifetime, they could see the tower which prized itself in gloom. There it was the tower of doom, Belle á Noir, in the land of - Moradiya. This was Morkann's dungeon of hell. This was the most dangerous of places of all where anyone would ever dare to visit. It was a flat, dry, and monotonous, seemingly limitless sand-mottled wasteland without landmarks or water or any other relief. This was visible for miles and miles. There was no motion; the flat, wide-open grains of sand danced on the solemn ground, bouncing off into the abyss.

This wasn't a Sahara-like desert of sand dunes. Instead there were sporadic open crevices; deep, dark purple boulders,

167

fallen fluorescent, crimson-colored stars, all weeping, with huge comets and half-withered long tails of misshapen rock.

Irregular bursts of orange-yellow flames and blue fire shot up into the atmosphere as far as the eye could see from atop the brown earthen crust of an old volcano. This was a surface that looked as hard as stone and was even less inviting.

James, still in deep thought, wondered about the events that had occurred, about his Mother metamorphosing into a just a simple beam of light. She had become a celestial creature; perhaps fitting quite easily into a storybook—one James would not have read.

He pondered still about Jambalee and of his wise words when remembering Princess Anna-Lisa: "Certain things will catch your eye, only pursue those who capture your heart, my dear James". "But did she capture my heart? I don't know, but I have got to find her, she hs got be in there, I am sure of it" he said to Jambalee, reassuring him.

James took in a deep breath, stooping cautiously as he passed the illuminated, fallen comets and wandering deep into the dark terrain led by a bright beam of light, which was now his Mother. The hope of light prevailed as he felt his Mother's presence.

Jambalee glanced over at James, just to see how he was coping with his Mother's appearance. He looked ahead and was able to see the deep lichen covered cove where Halaconia and the unicorn, together with the Centaurs, were waiting impatiently for the command to commence war with Morkann's ghouls, there were hundreds of creatures, which looked like wolves, and various Aras, constellation stars in the shapes of wild beasts—shimmering toward James. He had never seen and all these different sizes and shapes. "There they are! Look at them!" He pointed to the strong figures he was able to make out in the distance. Jambalee looked around and noticed that everyone suddenly stopped moving. The noise and babble diminished as their mass mutated slowly, becoming inaudible. They had become still, silently kneeling as Lindiarna approached in the image of a beam of golden light source around her.

Tom gave a broad smile, unaware that the beam of golden light he was now in view of was his Mother. James hugged his brother, but Tom rebuffed his affection. The creatures bowed in respect, for their Queen, Lindiarna, had returned.

"My humble ones, you have kept this land alive! We will regain in peace and valiant soldiers will succeed." The light source scaled the rugged terrain, shining brightly. The centaurs' statuesque strength became visible as they stood proud and prominent among the constellation and the army of Lupans.

Tom peered intently at Jambalee, as James realised the gold beam around his Mother was there for a reason, and he understood she may not be returning home alive as she was. But Tom became numb with disbelief that the beam of light he was now in view of, was indeed his Mother who had simply, silently, transformed into a golden beam of a light hologram. How could this be? He thought to himself. After all, he left her well and in control. "So…how?" muttered Tom in complete submission to anyone who would answer him. Now in turmoil, he turned to his brother, wanting to confirm that his beloved Mother had not died, but just changed her appearance until they all returned home. Tom with a grief stricken face tried to console himself.

Jambalee sucked in the air and inflated his small lungs, turning to face a distressed Tom, trying to console him. "Tom, your Mother is brave, and you must know she chose to return." Natalya wrapped her arm around him, lowering her gaze toward Tom. She tightened her lips, gripping his shoulder as she comforted him.

Jambalee, listening and watching intently, walked over to Tom. He endearingly offered, "Your Mother, Queen Lindiarna, chose to return to the Kingdom she had left behind. You must know this, young prince: when you look back, moments are never still, we can never store them. This was her destiny," Jambalee said. Tom was not able to restrain his sorrow; after all, his Mother had transformed to a golden bright light source.

The Unicorn, bowed his head as if he was bowing in respect toward the light, who was of course Lindiarna. Halaconia, Aspero, and the Lupans in attendance bowed to the beam of celestial light hovering beside them.

Tom turned quickly and gave a half smile, suppressing the rest of his tears "What's going on?" he asked.

Jambalee placed his hand onto Tom's bare forearm. Peering intently and trying to make sure he was ready to hear the rest of the news of his Mother's choice, he continued in a solemn tone. "My child, our Queen has returned. The doors of the Carbonite world have now closed forever for her." He placed his other little hand on Tom's shoulder. He began to pat it, trying to console him.

With teary eyes, Tom looked at Jambalee in despair. For that split second, he felt like Goliath. Tom's world collapsed in front of him with the enormity of the news he was hearing. "My Mom is she…" He was unable to articulate his words as his tears slowly fell like melted diamonds to the rugged ground and his stomach flip-flopped into a tight knot.

Tom stopped, suddenly realising his Mother was no more. He tried to understand the reason for his Mother returning to her galaxy. He still thought naïvely, or hoped that his Mother would return to Earth and that she would inevitably resume her normal state. Or would she?

Jambalee watched Tom's lips begin to quiver as he articulated the bad news that Lindiarna would never be able to return to the Carbonite, mortal world as his Mother in her normal state. Jambalee gently trying to console Tom calmly spoke, "Tom, you must be brave. I will always help you. You must know now that, as a mortal, the door of demise has been opened."

Tom's face plummeted, turning slightly grey in color as he listened intently to Jambalee. He froze, and his eyes dilated, he felt like his heart had stopped for a split second. There were no more tears left to fall, and his eyes became still, sore and red. He was gripped in a state of deep grief, and shock but just as quickly, his eyes darted toward the light source once more. It was then he could see Lindiarna in her golden light, the aura around covering her majestically. Her eyes glistened as Tom fought to be strong, suppressing his tears from his sore, dry eyes.

It was quite strange how everything had suddenly changed. There were a few moments previously, when he was waiting for his brother to arrive back. He was ecstatic, happy that everyone was to be reunited on the planets, but this moment was a complete illusion. Who knew that at this moment it would abruptly dissolve into complete disbelief and that he would feel that this was the last enchantment?

His Mother was now dead as a consequence of her arriving in her land, her body had gone, but her soul lived on. Tom became still and motionless as his tears slowly dripped on to his neck one by one from his tear-soaked amber eyes. He looked around at all the creatures and beings around him and then quickly back at his brother before he turned to his Mom, the light source. Through moistened eyes, he could see through the golden aura the hologram of light beaming in all its glory. He could see the figure of his Mother's appearance with her long, soft

Auburn hair brightly illuminating about her, like autumn shades of hope. His body felt heavy and his heart pounded like an elephant stampede.

"Oh man, why? But I can still see her? Was this my fault?" Tom questioned himself as he gripped his head in the enormity of what had happened. His face turned a ghostly pale shade, his eyes resembling glasses in a dishwasher—all steamed up.

His arms trembled as James approached him, wrapping his arms around his younger brother's shoulders. "It's going to be OK. The light lives on, Tom."

Tom instantly knew that James knew of his Mother's demise before he did and that his Mother was truly dead and that the enchantment was truly over.

James held Tom, consoling him the best way he could. They both understood that this was the final hurdle. Their Mother, Lindiarna, was no more. He stood completely still, staring in doe-eyed disbelief through James and all that was around him. He could understand that for that moment everything carried on, there was continuation. Life was dead, but the stars were still flickering and the Nebulas were still breaking around him.

Tom did not think his mind was empty. How could it be that on his return he would find his Mother no longer alive?. At that moment, his thoughts were like birds rattling around in a cage, fighting to escape.

James spoke, bravely trying to hold back his tears, while his voice began to falter slightly. "She knew it was a risk she wanted to take. She always had to return one day—we all have to—there is no such thing as immortality, hey? I suppose its all time and moments, and we had a wrong time with a bad moment."

Halaconia walked toward both boys, wrapping her arms around them. At that moment all were in an embrace that locked them together in their friendship for one another.

"No!" Tom bellowed, his scream reverberating off every comet and fallen star, making a loud droning noise. And then he remembered something he had seen when he first entered the planet, and suddenly, without thinking, he was running. He wasn't even sure that he was going in the right direction. Still in deep distress, everyone peered over to see Tom running.

He heard the clatter of something, with his eyes still water logged and his emotions in turmoil. He suddenly jumped up to stop Jambalee from. Jambalee was right behind him.

"I understand your anger, dear Tom, but you must know, Tom, dear Tom, that our Queen Lindiarna is not a Carbonite. And she would have had to leave some time. The force of Morkann's evil is far greater than we could ever imagine."

Tom rubbed his head, trying to make sense of everything that had been said to him.

"Our Queen will not return to the Carbon world with you again, Tom," said Jambalee.

Chapter IX
The Dominion Fall

Morkann's wrath was paramount. Her battle had commenced, with most of the planets trying to survive. It was gruesome. The Centaurs were slashing, striking, and killing, using the weapons against the deadly wrath of the horrific ghouls. Their rotating spokes, protruding dagger blades like a lion's tooth and with their spears like the entrance gates of hell, seemed too frightening and medieval, the thin ghouls who, with their malevolent faces of long, dead teeth, hollow eyes, and dark, blotchy, rough skin, with their uneven bone structure sliced the Lupans with sheer voracity. Aspero was able to see his defeat and did not wish to sustain any more of his army being slaughtered so he mounted on his beloved horse Ara. He sought his enemy and plunging his sword into Morkann's ghoul who dared confront him, dispersing a large, fan-shaped spray of blood, which oozed out in a liquid form high into the galactic air and falling onto the scrawny torsos of the ghouls and lost creatures. The battle was heroic and arduous. The deathly wailing and cries were so loud they would surely be heard on Earth. Aspero, the Lupan leader, and Chiron, Chief Centaur, were winning the fight of good, to save the dominion land but for how long?

Lindiarna was dead, and her being form was now just a light source a mere flame of light.

Aspero proudly rages war in the battlefield as he plunges his spear into one of Morkann's ghouls the galactic airspace is covered in red blood.

Chiron, the Centaur leading with Aspero in the battle ground for the Dominion land against Morkann's ghouls plunged his arrow into a deathly Morkannis.

James searched for an answer. His face was distraught, and his heart pounded with the anticipated horror before him. He glanced at his brother walking behind him, perhaps oblivious of the doom that was to unfold. Natalya stared at James in anticipation, her amethyst eyes sparkling like jewels she knew what was about to happen and how James would delve into the dark world. She raised her arm and pointed to the view in front of them. Would she, could she still help them through the darkness? She pondered.

James, still in anguish, walked toward Tom.

"Come on; you ok? It's just us two now," he said, trying to reassure his younger brother. Natalya smiled reassuringly and dipped her head as the two brothers headed on through the dense, barren, chalky terrain.

As they made their way back to join the others, the sky unexpectedly changed into a kaleidoscope of burning colors; yellow, orange, fuchsia, and pink all dazzling, revolving into a whirl until it transformed into a dark hole.

"Argh! Oh no!" screamed Tom. "Crikey! Where are you, the smoke is too strong? I can't see! What's happening?" shouted Tom.

Unable to see, the brothers tried to remain calm at the entrance to the gorge, but they were unable to sustain their balance then with the sudden revolving whirls of a star storm dust, it became harder. James's heartbeat thrummed against his ribcage, his mouth tasted like iron, and his breath caught in his throat. "Can you see Tom?" asked James.

"We have to go over there; Natalya said pointing to the volcanic ledge"

"Look out!" James bellowed as he propelled Tom away from pending the storm.

Tom suddenly felt the gush of a strong dust storm whirlwind zoom past him, navigating him into another labyrinth. Stretching out his arms to hold his balance, he was unable to pivot on the precarious ridge.

"Argh!" he yelled. "What is going on? What's happening?" He tried to take hold of the thick green vines floating suddenly around him. Everything zoomed too quickly all around, and he became puzzled and dazed. The hair on the back of his neck stood up like a porcupine's quills while his colour drained from his face. His sweat trickled down his neck and his throat became blocked with a sudden pressure. He closed his lips tightly.

"Tom, grab onto something, and keep your eyes shut!" James screamed and began throwing the thick vines around like they were skipping ropes.

Hearing his brother, Tom grabbed a large vine and watched as the green Nebula spat out a waft of ghostly images that whirled and swirled around him.

It was too late. A large meteor whizzed out of control, sparking shots of blue electricity, then erupting into millions of stars shooting wildly, as if out of a machine gun firing

The battle for the Dominion lands against Morkann's ghouls, led by fearfuless Aspero and Chiron the Chief Centaur

It was riotous. The Milky-Way lights flickered in every direction and the solar flames shot out like cannons dispersing light fuses on fire. The burnt amber rocks began to spew out everywhere, falling everywhere. Tom and James were caught in the warfare of stars. The crimson meteor ruptured and separated quickly, and then a sudden change occurred. The rocks splintered and cracked, forming a drop so deep and dark that the void dropped to hell itself. A light source suddenly exploded with a ferocious *boom*, and wild, blazing suddenly fires erupted in a fountain of colors, roaring with malicious flames and encapsulating all in its path.

James tried to open his eyes but could not see, for the fierce, burning fire was too bright, smoldering intensely and overpowering everything in its path into smithereens.

Some of the fragments would make their way toward Earth, burning up as they hurtled through the atmosphere, to form a meteoroid or into a bright shooting star. Larger meteors formed Morkann's fireballs, as they burned violently and then disintegrated until they evaporated into their path. Thunder and bolt of sharp blue light spurred and shot out, hitting the mountainous ridge where they all stood in a deep panic. James hugged onto the mountain ridge for dear life; the volcanic lava spewed everywhere in a kaleidoscope of colors, in the wildest shapes of Morkann and her evil medusa hair swaying in the images of raging fire. The flames roared high up into the gorge as James gripped on to the ledge as tightly as he was able. His face scorched by the intense heat given out. James began to feel it difficult to breathe as the heat from the flames intensified it became more forceful, raging shapes of hell below his feet. Natalya and Tom were held back by the intensity of the flames roaring up into the airspace as the volcanic mountain gorge separated. Feeling helpless they watched in horror as Morkann's inferno changed into every shade of ferocious flames.

James grips on to the burning ledge. His hands scored and burnt away from Morkann's flames as they roar out to attack him.

The mountain shuddered, releasing loose rocks, and then suddenly with a tumultuous boom, separated into two jaw-dropping spires that formed a drop to an open, blazing fire in a roaring oven. James stared at Tom in intense horror, he squeezed his eyes tightly, trying to squash the pain and heat away, to no avail. Again a sudden unbridled roar erupted, followed by a dull crack and loud thunder, letting out fumes of toxic sulfur and rampant, wild, raging flames of rainbow colors. The angry fire roared through the chasms jagged, newly created spires. The heat was too intense, and as Tom tried to peep through his squinted eyes, he could see holograms of Morkann sniggering maliciously through the giant flames.

"CLOSE YOUR EYES! Close your eyes, Tom! Tom, don't see her! Don't look at her!" James screamed, trying to grip onto the rock with his bare hands. Suddenly one of his hands started to slip from his grip, and he was unable to sustain his hold as the mountains began to separate sending debris tumbling into the cave of fire.

"No!" He screamed. James gripped on so tightly that his hands became red, and sore. They were put under so much strain that his knuckles protruded through his skin, as his face stretched in anguish and pain. James gripped with all his might onto the rock so that he would be with his brother, but it was no use. The heat from the flames seared like hell itself. The separation of the mountain into two spires was too great. James held on to the ledge as he watched the burning molten shapes fly out of the chasm.

Natalya, glided as near to James as she was able to trying to use her powers to elevate him out of the burning spire, but Morkann's evil power was too strong, and she was unable to stop the separation. The mountain rumbled and cracked with a tumultuous colossal boom. A chasm and a humungous gorge had been created with jagged spires emulating the doors to a hell opening its mouth like a cavern awaiting looming death. The blaze in iridescent red, yellow, orange and fierce blue flames roared and spat out piecing the galactic skyline in wild shapes of witches and ghouls trying to snatch whoever was near to them. It was like Morkann was preparing for the kill preparing for battle!

Now the brothers were separated on two jaw-breaking, spires, their screams and shouts were eaten by the curdling of molten lava and roaring of fire flames. Eventually James lost sight of both Tom and Natalya as the jagged wedge spire between them had too vast.

Tom screamed, holding back his tears of sorrow. He let out a raging growl, yet it was not to be heard. Suddenly alone, the sixteen-year-old turned in desperation to Natalya for guidance. His red sore eyes soaked in pain, he rubbed them as he turned away from the smoke and fury of orange and blue flames. "Where is he?"

Natalya dropped her head, appearing despondent. She knew where destiny would take James, but she was unable to reveal it.

"Tell me, you have to! He is my brother!" demanded Tom. Natalya gazed calmly into Tom's face, then placing her hand on his shoulder, said,

"Tom, you must be patient. I understand you are from the Carbon world, but this moment you are in will materialize out of great tribulation. You will see and feel the change to come. Know that James went forth to find his quest, and he will conquer and succeed. It is now that James will find his solace; you will see. Do not be afraid and do not be alarmed. He will survive!" Natalya levitated with a glow of soft white light around her. She then gently spoke in Latin: *"Et faciet, et prosperabitur, et sine ullo dolore, cupiditate ducti Victor."* (He will succeed without pain or greed and return victorious.)

Elevating toward Tom, Natalya stretched her long, thin arms shrouded in her silver sleeves out to him, her pale face taut as she peered closely into his soul.

"James will take care of himself; I know he can." Tom furrowed his eyebrows, spitting out the words to Natalya. He perished the thought of his brother being killed by the raging fire booming out between the newly created chasms. He snatched at the swaying, burnt vines that looked like spider legs protruding in front of him.

Watching Natalya Tom said, "Yes, but how do you know this? We are in a different part of the planets, and I know the war was raging when we left!"

Tom glared up at the tall, svelte figure, accepting her words of comfort. But he was still confused and worried for his brother. Totally alarmed, he glanced around him. Agonizing, the thought of James perhaps being killed! Tom quickly and anxiously shook his head, trying to change his thought pattern. He turned to Natalya again, in desperation to do something. Glaring up at the svelte figure with his teary eyes and angry face, he spoke, "James, can take care of himself. I know he can!" he said blurting out the words to Natalya. Glaring at her with his furrowed eyebrows, seeking some comfort.

Tom was distraught and still perishing the thought of his brother being killed by the raging fire roaring out between the newly created chasms. He tried to snatch again at the swinging, brown burnt vines that now looked like spiders legs protruding in front of him. In the turmoil Tom thought about his brother and Mother, his pain now etched upon his face. He pondered deeply, his eyes now wide and transfixed in thought, still holding on tightly to the swinging vine and jagged boulder he found himself next to. The burning rock with the volcanic mountain wedge becoming vast as it separated.

James was in anguish and confused, distraught he called out his brother's name in vain. "Tom, Tom...where

ARE you?" James bellowed from the top of his voice, squeezing his eyes and dodging the smoldering molten lava and broken comets falling around him.

It was no use; although James hollered, his voice rumbled through the void. At the top of his voice, he tried again and again, the deathly separation of the two towering spires simply absorbing his voice. James held his head thinking of his brother alone and his Mother dead, becoming a mere light source. Grimacing and frowning, he rubbed his head in despair.

"How will we stop her wrath? What must we do?" He knew it was Morkann causing the war and the dominion of evil in the form of the volcanic mountain. Come on. I have got to get out of here, he thought to himself. The rocks continued to splinter and fall, breaking into a rhythm of haiku, pitter-patter pit / pitter pat / pit-pit-pat patter. The dwindling of rocks sounded to a slow tempo, intensifying while allowing the rocks and stones to perforate the ground as they shattered into a thousand pieces for some time, until it slowed down completely. It was almost as if it were urgently trying to communicate a message to him. He clasped his ears tightly, to protect them from the raucous sound of the falling rocks. His mouth stretched across his face in pain and anguish.

"This must be a trick or something; it's got to be," James muttered to himself in despair. He stared, gawping at the mountain as it began to change its shape. It groaned and let out a tumultuous thunder. The rugged, craggy mountain slowly began to separate from the others, rupturing and causing heavy debris to fall again. A fury of brightly colored angry flames roared while thick, vibrant, boiling lava spewed over the ridge between the two voids, only to explode into shards of a vibrant inferno. James clung onto the jagged mountain rock, his hands and face becoming uncomfortable and red in the heat. The glow of the fire forced him to hold onto the rock ledge stronger as the heat scorched his face. He squinted his eyes as he peered through to see the flames lunging at him and Morkann's image leering and sniping at him through the raging lava

Murmuring broken words in pain, breathing heavily, and moaning in anguish, James realized he had now entered Moradiya, a dark demonic land and that there was much evil—with its origin—around him.

He stood proud and nervous on the thrusting spires of pure, naked rock that shot into the galactic airspace so high that it was hard to believe the very Milk Way hadn't been perforated. The boys and Natalya peered at each other intently, their bug eyes fixated on what was about to happen. A deep shadow swept over the huge jagged mountain edges, then a sudden rumble and thunder roared before the mountain rock begun to cascade in two spires around them.

James clung onto the jagged spire rock with all his might, grabbing the sharp rock he yelled out to his brother, "Quick, hold onto something—argh! Tom…"

Natalya quickly grabbed Tom and pulled him away onto the second spire protecting him from the burning roaring molten lava. They watched helplessly in horror as James struggled to hold onto the separated jagged mountain spire.

He was trying to cling onto the rock with his bare hands, fighting with the roaring flames and barely clutching the jagged, rock that tore at his skin. His hands became sore and blood-oozed out of his fingers. His red hands were now saturated with sweat, blood and heat from the furnace of flames roaring through the volcanic mountain. His veins now protruding like arteries as his knuckles seemed too eager to escape from his hands. He wasn't really sure what was happening as he tried to scan the furnace and spire for his brother or Natalya, but James was in so much pain. He suddenly spotted a figure through the roaring flames and tried in vain to capture Natalya's attention as she hovered around Tom, protecting him from the fierce blaze. They were unable to see James precariously pivoting from the ledge. The wild flames with bubbling molten lava were too bright and strong that with a crack in the crust a boiling lava lake was formed. It snaked its way through the single spire forming a hot moat of effervescing lava. James saw his brother with Natalya for a split second and then he did not. The plumes of smoke and dust from the heat of the burning lava turned everything into an open oven of hell. His body trembled and his heart pounded as if to escape from his torso. He was drenched in heat and sweat, his hair stood up, sizzling from the roaring flames trying to catch it and set it alight and his lips became dry. He was petrified, scared for his life. Now he was stranded alone in a weird world, caught between hell and the spikey, jagged, demonic mountaintop. His distraught mouth stretched as he contemplated his fate, pondering on how to get out of the mountain dagger formation he found himself in and to fulfill what he came to do, which all now seemed impossible.

James, trying to glance all around him, peering into the crimson void beyond, scrunched his eyes away from the roaring, blazing, brightly colored flames. In the alien landscape hiding amid the baking rocks and between the flashing asteroids, there was a sense of menace, like the purr of a puma feasting on its prey; Morkann was never far away with her banshee wailing fighting through the flames. She was lurking within the molten lava and she here for a purpose. However, Natalya continued to try and protect Tom from the heat. James relentlessly tried to seek out Tom or Natalya through the raging incandescent flames and flashing lights of the broken and burnt stars, with the lava spilling over the separated mountain peaks.

Raising her voice, Natalya shouted, "Tom watch out!" as she sucked in her prominent cheeks from the horror she was witnessing. "Your brother...Tom, do not be afraid. It is the origin of evil, and sometimes we face the darkness. If we are strong, we will succeed, and we will see the light.

Come; we must return to the battle that Morkann has erupted in the valleys of Moradiya," she ordered. "Tom, you must comprehend this: James will survive and succeed in his quest," she said reassuringly, taking Tom by his shoulder away from the raging mountain covered in burning, roaring flames. "The dominion is separating, and Morkann will apply any peril she can to entice you to death. We have go from here!" Natalya insisted. They could see a dark shadow sMothering the mountain before sulphuric green acid was seen sliding down the mountain side before a loud rumbling was heard and the dominion mountain began to crack and split, plumes of smoke and dust emerged, while wild flames roared inside the mountain the molten lava wept through the crevices. It was riotous and frightening. Tom, helplessly watched in horror as his brother was now alone,

James was struggling to cope with the flames as he pivoted upon the burning ledge. His memories jumped all around him like muggers, confused and frustrated in the range of darkness, flickering through each incandescent flame. His anguish was chiseled upon his face.

He tightly squeezed his ocean-soaked eyes, trying to stare through the burning mountain as much as possible, but it was too difficult. He could see the flames wail and roar, scorching furiously, recognizing it as Morkann. He could see that the eye of the enemy Morkann was moving all around him, throwing the flames at every angle, lashing its fear in every direction. His hand gripping the ledge was throbbing and had turned red in agony. His whole body converted in to a statue, locking in a stiff position. He dropped his head and managed to glance below at his feet. There it was, the cause of his struggle—Temperatia, the wrath of Morkann had arrived in evil herself. She was shrieking, her strands of slithering serpent hair wafting and floating in the lava sea.

Her wrath was now abundant, with her hologram floating in a soft black drizzle, tormenting James through the bubbly lava in an eerie rhythm.

James froze in horror, with the knowledge of Morkann creating the wrath to destroy the mountain he precariously stood upon. A deep dark shadow crept down the mountain blocking all the light from the constellation above. James and Tom were aghast watching with Natalya in disbelief. A tumultuous rumble was heard, then a sudden thud cracking and rumbling with great plumes of smoke and dust appear out of which hot molten lava began to creep out of the mountain in the image of Morkann's ghouls. Natalya suddenly took hold of Tom as she saw in a plume of smoke and dust the mountain began to split into two jagged spires slowly separating. Natalya grabbed Tom and pulled him toward her, whilst James was left on the other side of the rising sun, she frowned in despair having to immediately leave if they were to survive. Lindiarna, light beam tried to glow across the lava lake, but to no avail as her light was too weak against the demonic shapes created by the flames of fury. The time passed, and the fire and lava slowly diminished, leaving only short, sharp sparks of light flashes, with the sound of Morkann's banshee wailing occurring intermittently, fading away until it finally became settled and sporadic. James clung onto the blade of rock with his bare hands with all his might. As the minutes turned to hours, James lost sight of his brother and Natalya.

He scanned the tor wildly in desperation trying to see his brother together with Natalya, yet he now began to realize that he was trapped in chasm of solitude and in a pyroclastic, burning, crevasse with racing avalanches of scorching rising molten and lava. The explosive volcanic ash splashed out of the spire, trying to escape but was held back as the shadow of doom drifted across the terrain. These golden sulphuric acid spurges fell sporadically around the mountain, annihilating any form of life. James would now find his quest in solitude he was where darkness dominated the malevolent, desolate galaxy, but he had to stay alive.

Realising his plight and clinging to the ridged volcano ledge, James decided to try to disembark from the ledge and navigate to find assistance from whoever would be able to help him.

Gripping the remnants of the precipitous spire, he carefully began to release his each finger from his grip. His sore hand began to pound angrily. The flames roared back in anger and fury, enticing James to jump away in fear. Still the scorching hot amber lava, with the embers flickering, propelled out of the volcanic mountain spire toward James.

He began to carefully and precariously lift himself out of the jagged spire. He was dicing with the treacherous fire and iridescent flames blazing all around him. Death was certainly in his cards. Now totally unaccompanied, James pondered on how and where he would start to walk away from the deathly gorges of Moradiya, but as he tried to view his route, the heat from the mountain inferno was too much to bear and he fell to the ground. The fate of the worlds he found himself in became more apparent. The dominion of evil around him grew even stronger. The union of the volcanic mountain had been separated, and Morkann, had her intent to disperse her sinister evil darkness and perilous ways to the beings and surviving creatures, which now included James. His fate had fallen into an unseen danger that lay before his new journey.

His face stretched in anguish and turmoil. "Natalya! Tom!" He bellowed to no avail.

His screams and yells could not be heard, they were lost among the sounds of the Lava Lake curdling and molten rock spewing everywhere. Now he found himself totally alone in an unforeseen world. As he sat down on the charred terrain against a rock which had not been burnt away from the molten lava, he grimaced scanning the journey before him.

Then suddenly a blinding light source appeared enticing him to cover his eyes in haste, "Who is it?" he said squeezing his eyes tightly.

"It is I, your mortal Mother, Queen Lindiarna. James, your brother and Natalya are well they have gone to the other planet Oblivionarna. The Unicorn is with Princess Anna-Lisa, and they await your return. You must cross this rift and go and rescue the Princess". James rubbed his eyes in disbelief as he tried to glare into the light source.

"Mom! Is that you?" James asked excitedly, trying to stand on the charred ash. "Mom!" he bellowed, "is that you? You have to speak to me again - Mom!"

The light diminished slowly leaving just, embers of molten lava simmering around him. He quickly turned around to see if he was able to view the light source once more, but it was too late, Lindiarna had gone leaving behind an instruction for him to always follow the light. James, became morose, he dipped his head in despair not knowing if he would ever see his brother or Mother again. His face was distraught and his mind pensive, he looked down at his hands, they were still sore and scorched, he felt helpless. In anguish James turned to the horizon in front of him, in some hope he would be rescued. However, he quickly realised he was not on planet Earth, who could it be that would take him back home. James was in turmoil; his eyes became water logged as he ried to hold back his tears. In total disarray, he glared out at the remnants of the jagged spire of where his brother once beckoned in anguish. They had vanished; there was no sign of Tom or Natalya. The commotion of the volcanic mountain, separating had ceased and James now stood alone.

Dictionary of Charismas

This is to introduce you to the pronunciation and dictionary of words used in this book.

A
Aspero – Latin name for Purple Gerbera.
Lead solider of Lupan army. Strong and powerful.
Pronunciation:- Ass-per-row (Fiction)
Ara - Strong
This is a southern constellation situated between Scorpius and Triangulum Austral. Its name is Latin for "altar". Ara was one of the 48 Greek constellations described by the 2nd century astronomer Ptolemy
B
Basilisk – Serpent

Legendary creature — used in many books.
From the Greek βασιλίσκος basilískos, "little king;" Latin regulus) is a legendary reptile reputed to be king of serpents and said to have the power to cause death with a single glance. The Basilisk of Cyrene is a small snake, "being not more than twelve fingers in length and is very venomous. It leaves a wide trail of deadly venom in its wake. It's gaze is likewise lethal.
Pronunciation : bas-uh-lisk
C
Chiron

Greek mythology, Legend
Chiron was notable throughout Greek mythology for his youth-nurturing nature. His personal skills tend to match those of Apollo, his foster father and sometimes Artemis legend.
Pronunciation:- she-ron
Cepheus — *King of Ethiopia. A constellation near the north celestial pole is named as Cepheus.* **(fact)**
Pronunciation:- Sef-fee-ass (*fiction*)
D
Dillyans — *Female version of Imp type creature has pink hair and sliver transparent wings.* (*fiction*)
Pronunciation: Dil-ye-ans.
G
Galzar — *A fictional character of great mystical power. A Shaman from the other world of good.*
H
Hakeem- *Enormous, Huge as Redwood Coast Tree. Good spirit*
to aid family. Resides and hides in appearance as mountain in Oblivionarna. (fiction)
Arabic word for healer -**fact**
Appearance — *When seen displays in Gregorian monk robe. Face not visible.*
Pronunciation: Ha- keem.
Halaconia — **Latin** *for Ginger Lilly*
Appearance - *Hooved Dillyan with ginger-lilies adorning right side of her cheek and neck. Her long aubergine curly hair covers seductively. She has strong silver transparent wings. Good Spirit.*
(fiction)
Pronunciation: Hal-ee-cone-nia
I
Iktomi — Wisdom **(fact legend)**
Tribal affiliation: Sioux
Is the son of the Rock, a god creator. Iktomi is the trickster figure of the Lakota, Dakota, and

200

Nakota Sioux tribes.
He is usually depicted
as a human man in
Sioux legends. Iktomi
is a negative role model.
Iktomi's folly is more
serious and violent, and the
stories become cautionary
tales about the dangers of
the world.
Pronunciation:- eek-toh-
mee

J

Jambalee – *Leader of the Imps
Oblivionarna. He is the only imp
that has feet.* **(fiction)**
Pronunciation: Jam-bal-ee
Appearance: - Small and
round with strange hair
protruding out from his
oversized winding hat.
His tweed tail coat is held
together with a single
brown button.
He is a loyal servant to
the court of Princess
Lindiarna.

L

Lupans – Imp type
creature. They are the only
ones that have hoofs for
feet. Strong and loyal.
(Fiction)
Pronunciation: Loo-pans
Lindiarna – Princess of
Oblivionarna
Daughter of King Cepheus.
(fiction)
**Pronunciation: Lin-di-
arn-a**

M

Magellanic clouds – Two
diffuse luminous patches
on the southern sky, now
known to be irregular
galaxies that are the closest
to Earth. **(fact)**
Pronunciation: - Mag-gel-
lan-ic
Morkannis – Abhorrent
Ghouls soldiers with
allegiance to King
Polydectes; only found in
Moradiya. **(fiction)**

Pronunciation: Mor–kan-nis

Moradiya —A name of an irregular demon shaped planet. **(fiction)**

Pronunciation: More–rad-di- a

Morkann — Tyrant wicked princess, Daughter of King Polydectes. **(fiction)**

Pronunciation: More-can

O

Oblivionarna: - *one galaxy luminous patch on the southern sky, known to be an irregular shape.* (*fiction*)

Pronunciation:-Obli-vi-arna

P

Polydectes— (based on legend character)

In Greek mythology, Polydectes is who this character is based on. He wanted revenge so that he could marry his love. **(fact)**

Pronunciation:- poly-ec-tees

Prytaneum -In ancient Greek, a public hall of a Greek state or city, in which a sacred fire was lit. This Court entertained successful foreign ambassadors. **(fact)**

Pronunciation:-Pry-tan-e-um

T

Typhoeusina: Derived from Greek word Typhoeus in Greek mythology. It is a monster with a hundred serpent heads, born to Tartarus and Gaia after the Titians defeated by Zeus. **(fact - legend)**

U

Uroboros — A circular symbol depicting a snake or less commonly a dragon. **(fact)**

Pronunciation: you- row - borrows

U-Targ – Scandinavian
mythology home of giants.
(fact)
**Pronunciation: You-targU-
Targ** –

About the Author

Rayner Tapia is the author of the series The Adventures of Tom McGuire. She started writing this fantasy/sci-fi book series because she wanted to share some of her stories and the joy she has with words.

Before writing this series, she was involved in teaching English and computers at various educational and financial institutions for many years.

Rayner lives in London with her family. Her hope is that you enjoy the book and the worlds created.

Printed in Germany
by Amazon Distribution
GmbH, Leipzig